Sara's Adventures

Sara's Adventures

SUSAN KAY BOX BRUNNER

Published by FWB Publications, Columbus, Ohio 43207

Published in the United States of America
ISBN: 978-1-940609-77-5
Fiction / Family Life
16.06.07

For all the generations of women and men before and including that of my mother, Laura, and my father, John, and to all the generations that come afterward. May we each be thankful for God and our heritage, for without it, we would not exist.

ACKNOWLEDGMENTS

The author wishes to acknowledge the following people for helping bring this book to light.

Mandy Larger, librarian, who fixed errors and advised on the sections needing rewriting for clarity and grammatical help.

Gail Tipton-Castle, photographer and co-supporter, with Christie Burke-Crawford and Magi Lawson.

To my brother Thomas; my husband, Larry; my children Marica, Bobette, Khelisa, James, Mark, and Victor; my grandchildren Christa, Sueann, Anthony, Mahlon, Sophia, and Sylvia; and great-granddaughters Riley, Khloe, Karleigh for their encouragement and loyal support.

I don't think they realize just how unachievable it would be to bounce back and stay afloat without them.

1

The double-engine aircraft, carrying 173 passengers, began circling the airport.

Sara News noticed the clouds were separating and showing promise of a bright new sunny day. It was then a passengers' sign flashed and read, "Passengers, take your seat now, and buckle up."

A crackling noise was heard, and Sara's stomach took a plunge. She quickly realized it was coming from the intercom.

"Due to the amount of air traffic, we will need to hover above the airport for about forty-five minutes longer," the senior pilot announced. "The tower will contact me when it is acceptable for our entrance."

A hushed moment passed.

"Attention, attention, everyone," the pilot went on, using his baritone voice. "Headsets for music are now available and are free. Just ask one of our Gray Stewards for them."

Sara reached for a feathered pillow, which was provided to the passengers, from the overhead shelving. She placed it behind her head and leaned into it for some much-needed rest.

For a moment, she touched the penny swear necklace her dear friend Karen had given her while they were still in high school. It willed her to calm down. Just the thought of their promises made to each other brought a smile to Sara's lips and a satisfaction in knowing they would always be there to help one another.

Her youngest child, Matthew, began to squirm while seated in her lap. She readjusted the narrow seat and rubbed Matthew's back to settle him down.

Sara glanced in Timmy's direction. He, being her firstborn, was trying to peek through the small window by his seat. His eyes were wide and stretched open. "I can't see anything, Mom."

Sara smiled and patted his hand when she saw the foggy window. She watched him twist in his seat, muttering, "Now no one can see."

She poked Timmy and handed him a book from her purse.

Sara's mind began to wander, as her eyes fluttered and finally closed. One question kept nagging, and it persisted: how long had it been since she was last in Ohio?

Guilt crept over her once again as she repeated the shocking words from the letter she had carefully folded and placed in her skirt pocket.

My dearest Sara,

I'm writing this to you. It concerns your father. My Paul has slipped away. He passed Tuesday morning in his sleep, and he appeared to be at peace.

You know from my former letter he had taken an uncontrollable fall from his wheelchair. The accident left him with a fractured right hip. The doctor advised him to have a complete hip replacement. And he did agree, and had the surgery. At first, the hip replacement seemed quite successful, but Paul's body, after several weeks, rejected the foreign material. His hip area just wouldn't heal correctly.

Sara blinked as she continued reading.

Sara, the infection spread so quickly it caused your father to have a serious setback. He continued to become weaker as the weeks went on. It was within three weeks until pneumonia set into his body, making the lung function harder for your dad to breathe. Although the doctor prescribed special breathing treatments, it totally zapped him of what little strength he had gained. His energy level got depleted, and he was then ordered back into the hospital. He was only there for a short while because Dr. March, the family doctor, felt Paul would do better under a total Nurse's Care, so he sent your dad home.

Sara, honey, Paul had only been home ten days. He was adjusting to his new schedule and was doing as well as could be expected. He even joked some. The doctor also ordered a new chair for Paul, straight from the factory. It had a special foam six inches thick, and was placed on the bottom seat. The back had a curve that was lined with foam to ease the pressure points his body suffered. The chair was made for him to avoid any pain. His chair was covered with a nonallergic fabric so it would not cause him other issues with his breathing.

The Nurse's Care unit placed his chair in our living room by the bay window, overlooking the rolling wildflower meadows he so dearly enjoyed.

The two assigned Nurses Care unit ladies lifted your father into the specially designed chair one early morning, around five. He was having devotions in John, and while sitting there, he appeared to have dozed off. I thought he had gone to sleep, but instead, he had passed away.

Sara, finding him dead was such a shock. Dear, you know I've always tried to be prepared, but honestly, Sara, this time, it left me in a state of being quite the opposite. I know the truth; he is in a far better place now, without his pain, and I know his being with the One he believed in is comforting, but I honestly still feel so lost.

Paul was my best friend, and after all these years together, well, I loved and miss him so very much, and I always will.

Thinking about this again brought on a tremor. Sara felt her father's death all over. She began to violently shake within her inner soul and spirit. She covered her mouth, quickening a gasp. She willed aside the knowing and its effect and the toll his death had taken on her physically. The uncontrollable tears formed in her eyes. She touched her cheek and felt a tear drop. She sighed, and the tears flowed right after another.

She recalled how sick she had been with the flu. Her doctor prescribed an antibiotic, but it was late with taking any major effect. The flu became so awful she had been placed under quarantine. She was not permitted to venture outside her house, nor was anyone allowed to enter. She had to totally wait for the doctor's release stating she had a full bill of good health and was free from the flu bacteria. Sara was so glad her children had had their flu shots just two weeks earlier along with her husband, Ken.

It was terrible not being able to fly home to her mother's after she received the initial phone call stating her father had passed away. A deep sadness welled up in a hidden part of her heart. She had prayed and hoped for a time of healing, or at least for her pain to be eased.

Her mother had ended her call with, "I'll write you more on this matter later, for I just wanted you to know now about your father's passing. I'll be praying for you to get better, Sara, and hopefully, you can come home soon to see me. You know He'll carry us through this, Sara."

As the telephone went dead, she felt so helpless knowing her mother had to bear all the responsibilities of the service herself.

Two months dragged by. Ken and the boys were saved from the flu, and Sara's quarantine had been lifted. Ken had to operate his banking and farm business, and insisted she make plans for her and the children to leave for Ohio.

The call was made, and her boys were excited and expected to see their grandmother, Florence, although she went by her middle name, Louise.

The pilot's voice jolted over the speaker, which brought Sara back to reality.

"Stay seated, everyone," the pilot announced in his deep moderate tone. "We should be landing shortly. The landing gear is in place. We're just waiting for the signal. It shouldn't be too bumpy."

Sara noticed Timmy was fidgeting. He was having trouble sitting in his seat. He held his hands in a tight grip. He licked his mouth, anticipating the landing of the plane.

Looking at Matthew, she saw he had fallen asleep, and she felt that was a blessing in disguise.

Sara held her breath as the plane began to glide. The plane tipped forward and rocked, but it landed just fine. She let out a sigh of relief that the two boys and she had finally arrived in one piece.

Sara ushered them near the front revolving doors at Port Columbus International Airport. She stood holding one now-wide-awake child. Matthew began bouncing on her hip. She stared at Timmy while he pulled at her purse. She breathed in and ushered a prayer, *Thanks for riding with us.*

Sara stretched on her tiptoes to look for Karen, her best friend. She frowned. Had it been three and a half years since they had last seen each other?

Giving a panoramic view seeing the clock strike midmorning. Sara noticed the airport was already heavy with traffic. She was fascinated with all the bustling around with people coming and going to their different destinations, but it was hard for her to keep track of her children and continue to look for Karen at the same time.

Karen received a phone call. "Hello, Sara, is that you?" She was jumping up and down. "How are you?"

"Better now, thanks." A giggle slipped out. "I'm coming to Columbus."

"You are?" Karen exclaimed. "When?"

"I'll be there in two weeks. Can you come and pick me up?"

"Sure, I'll be there. You're flying? Friend, I can't wait to see you. Call me before you leave."

The line went dead, and Karen thought more on what Sara had mentioned. *She would be spending time with her mom, and she planned to visit her father's grave site. Hoping for some closure.*

Karen twisted her apron. What was up with that?

Didn't Sara know there wasn't any grave site?

Sara did sound excited to see Jud and, of course, her. She mentioned the need to see Jud about her new business enterprise. Sara had a joyful laugh when she spoke. "Karen, I'm going to be an entrepreneur!"

Karen shook her head in disbelief about Sara's going to her father's grave site. What was this "new adventure" Sara had rattled on about? Karen shrugged. Only time would tell. Karen knew she would just have to wait and see.

Karen recalled how Sara was always scared to fly. She would pray. Karen made sure she asked Sara to wear her old penny swear friendship necklace. She told her she would wear hers. Karen knew it sounded stupid, but it seemed to soothe her in iffy times.

A new anxiety settled in. Karen scouted for her necklace, and rummaged through a box from her closet. Holding it up, Karen smiled as she replaced the lid on the silver wooden box and returned it to the top shelf. Clutching the necklace, she quickly bowed her head and whispered,"

"Watch over Sara, please, and thank You."

Two weeks passed. Karen managed to maneuver through all the people at the airport. She stood with her hands on her hips. She somehow had missed Sara. She huffed as she rushed to the front information counter and had Sara paged. She stood on her tiptoes, and soon saw Sara. She was standing at the entrance. They had passed each other. Karen jumped up and down, waving her arms, trying to get Sara's attention. It took Sara a few minutes, and then their eyes met.

Karen saw Sara had plunked a carbon copy of Timmy on the other hip as she raised her free hand and waved back in acknowledgment.

Karen's twins had stayed with their father, Jud. He had volunteered to stay home and be with Luci and Luke so she could drive to the airport by herself and meet up with her friend Sara.

At their meeting, both ladies began talking at the same time and then found themselves laughing. They noticed things had not really changed between them over the past few years. Nodding, they both agreed. They were still the best of friends.

Karen's eyebrow lifted in question. She was surprised to see Sara holding a younger boy who noticeably looked a lot like Little Timmy. She glanced at Timmy. "You are filling out, and look how tall you've gotten."

Karen watched Sara laugh.

"Karen, meet Matthew," Sara said. "Girlfriend, we have a lot to catch up on."

"Hopefully in a little while," Karen answered. "You'll have my full attention. Maybe after the boys are down for a nap, or does Timmy still take one?"

"He still lies down, and sometimes, he falls asleep."

"I sure hope the twins, Luci and Luke, agree about their nap today and stay out of trouble. They were so hyped up when I left them with Jud." Karen let a slight laugh escape.

It set off a trickle until they both shared looks between themselves as only mothers could do in the moment.

Karen motioned. "Follow me, Sara."

The boys tagged along to look for the luggage. Karen pointed. "This way." Since she had picked Jud up at the airport recently, she knew where the new baggage bins were located. Going down to the third level was different, and it became a real challenge with handling the boys.

Karen and Sara noticed the escalator, as did Timmy. He jerked his hand free from his mom's and bolted toward the steps. Karen plunged forward, grabbed Timmy by the shirttail, and tried to keep him from skipping down the steps. "Timmy, whoa, buster! We'll do this together."

Hand in hand, Karen and Timmy moved. They placed their feet on the top step of the escalator, and it moved downward to the appointed destination.

Seeing Sara shifting Matthew from one arm to the other and from hip to hip made Karen declare, "He looks like a big bag of potatoes twisted in your arms."

Sara shifted her handbag to the other arm. "He's heavy."

"I'm sure he is. He seems taller than Timmy did at that age."

"He took his height from his dad."

Karen flagged her hand. The sign indicated they were on the third level. "Sara, I'll watch both boys while you retrieve the suitcases."

"Thank you," Sara said, smiling.

They decided the stairway was safer for them to tackle. Three flights later, they were at the exit.

Karen had brought the old reliable green two-toned four-door station wagon, with a raccoon tail dangling from the antenna, to pick Sara up from the airport. When they made it outside, Karen lifted her hand and pointed. "My station wagon is not much to look at, Sara, but it runs like a top. I had to park in the back. Third row. See it?"

Nodding, Sara smiled while walking with the boys.

Karen rattled on. "The twins' car seats are still in the vehicle. I had planned for Timmy to ride in one of them, but now, the other twin's car seat will come in handy for three-year-old Matthew."

Karen looked on as Sara made the necessary car seats' adjustments and placed her boys in the seats. "It won't be long now till we get to Karen's and Jud's place."

Timmy cried with glee while Matthew, watching him, clapped his hands.

Karen turned. "All aboard?" She saw the signal from Sara, and she slowly put the vehicle into drive. She was now on the road headed for Jud's and her house.

"Sara, the back roads are still the fastest way in traveling this time of day." Karen punched Sara. "Look in the backseat."

Karen watched as Sara turned. They had not traveled very far before Matthew was asleep.

Timmy began working his hands and feet against the front seat.

"What's the matter, Timmy?" Karen asked.

"Hurry up, Karen, I have to potty," Timmy answered.

"Okay, little man, hang on." Karen searched for the road sign saying "Rest Area." She pointed ahead, seeing it, and turned on the blinker, pulling in.

Sara took Timmy to the restroom while Karen stayed in the car attending to the sleeping Matthew.

Timmy hands were wet, and he was shaking them as he climbed in. "Karen?"

"What, little man?"

"Thank you." He buckled up and pointed. "Mom, shut the door. Let's go. Luke and Luci will be waiting on us."

Karen's smile broadened. She placed her left arm out the window and slowly eased onto the road once again.

They all sat in silence, only smiling at each other as they headed toward her place.

2

Jud kept fanning the door. Jud's head bobbed in and out the door while watching for Karen to pull into the driveway. He heard the horn, and came running outside to greet them. He also lifted an eyebrow when another little boy climbed down from the station wagon. Both boys smiled and instantly ran into Jud's welcoming arms.

He observed Sara as she gasped, crossing her arms, and her voice carried as she whispered to Karen, "I miss my husband, Ken, already."

Jud and Karen noticed she wiped at a tear sliding down her cheek. Karen slipped her arm around Sara's shoulder and gave her a little squeeze. "He'll miss you too."

Jud commented as he looked at the ladies, "You two seemed to still be able to read each other's minds, maybe even better now after all your time apart." He looked at Karen then Sara as they touched their necklaces at the same time.

"There's some mac and cheese and hot dogs in the kitchen waiting. The pan is full also, on low." Jud opened the door, carrying in their luggage. "They're just waiting on us to eat." He served ketchup on the side, in case they wanted to dip their hot dog on something.

Everyone hurriedly sit and ate. The roar of voices tried to override each other.

Timmy said, "It hit our empty spot, Jud," as he patted his stomach.

The boys gave Jud a two-thumbs-up for their meal. Smiling, Jud excused himself, staying in the large eat-in kitchen to sweep, mop, do the dishes, and take out the trash.

Sara heard him whistle as he worked, and made the comment, "You sure seemed content nowdays."

Karen was thrilled she had asked Jud to take the entire day off from work. She knew he still enjoyed his work, and he acted as if he was married to it, but he placed her first. Karen watched as he helped and interacted with Timmy and Matthew.

Timmy yawned. Luke put his arm around him. Luci mothered Matthew.

Karen showed them to their room and read to the four children. It wasn't long until they were down for a nap and asleep. She hoped it was for a very long time.

"Karen, can I borrow the green bomber?" Sara asked. "I would like to go see Mother."

"Sure, Sara, the keys are in it." Karen waved. "We'll watch the kids. They'll be fine."

"Thanks."

Although Sara was meditating on her journey, she still couldn't help being amused at the sight of the station wagon. It was old and a bit rusty, but why the tail? Sara adjusted the long front seat and excelled the pedal. The vehicle coughed, and black smoke rolled out from underneath in a cloudy pillar. She waited for a few seconds, and the engine warmed up—it purred.

She soon arrived at her mother's house. Sara admired the cherry finish on the door, where she stood knocking.

Mother should be home, she thought. *I hope she is surprised.*

"Come in."

Sara pushed the heavy door open and found her mom busy bustling around in the kitchen. She was making way too much dinner. She always did.

Sara looked at her mother's lined face. Louise seemed open-hearted when she held out her arms and surrounded Sara. Louise squeezed her daughter as if there would be no tomorrow. Sara hugged back and did little to move from her mom's arms. It felt comforting and welcoming—a long-overdue one. It was wonderful.

They both sat in the kitchen, one hand over the other.

"Sara, how are you doing?" Louise began. "Really?" She waved her hand. "It's so good to have you home. I've missed you and Timmy, and now there is little Matthew. It will be great to meet him. I can't wait to see them." Louise couldn't stop talking. "How is Ken doing? Is he ahead of the rainy season?"

Sara smiled and shook her head. She watched her mother ramble on.

Their eyes locked.

Hesitating, Louise spoke. "Sorry, Sara. I love you, and seeing you here is such a great gift."

Sara's smile increased. She folded her hands and bowed her head. *Thanks.*

Lifting herself up, she rested a hand on her mother's shoulder. "It's good to see you too, Mom." She took a mug of hot tea and slowly answered each one of her mother's questions. She began with how she was really doing.

"Mom, the news you were trying to relate over the phone about Dad's death came across so broken," Sara said. "The lines hissed, cracked, and faded our voices until our call ended." She stood, pacing on the floor and crossing her arms. "It was awful. I couldn't make a phone call out, nor could anyone's calls be received. The lines were down." She shook her head. "Another Mississippi storm passed through."

Louise nodded, patting Sara's back.

"The next day, the mailman came and left a letter from you," Sara went on. "I couldn't wait to read it, so I unfolded into the closest chair on the porch. As I read your explanation about Dad's death, it helped me to understand and better cope. You filled in a lot of missing gaps." Sara pressed a hankie to her eyes. "Mom, will you show me where he was last sitting?"

As if given an order, her mother moved from the room and walked to the bay window. She waved her hankie. "He was sitting right there." She pointed. "Come in, and we'll sit a spell."

Sara joined her mother, and they sat on the bench under the bay window. Sara reached and stroked her dad's Bible and let out a long sigh.

The room was silent, and quietness took over. Only tears from both ladies were shed.

Sara spoke slowly. "Mom, may we go to the cemetery now? I'm hoping his grave site will give some closure. It may come."

Her mom, with red-rimmed eyes, shook her head. "No, Sara."

Sara's head jolted and, in a higher–pitched voice, asked, "Why not?"

Louise's lips thinned and whitened as through gritted teeth she said, "Your father is not buried in a cemetery."

Sara clasped her hands to her chest. "What? Well, where is he?"

Her mom fingered her apron as she frowned. "Sara, Paul never wanted to be viewed at a funeral home. He had told me along time ago. He said, 'I know people only by their-my living. I have never heard from anyone that was dead.' And he was serious when he spoke. He added, 'Louise, don't you let people stare down at me.'"

Louise let out a hoarse laugh. "Bless his soul. He never lost that off sense of humor. He made me promise. If he were to go first, he made me swear to have him cremated."

Sara crossed her arms. "Well, why didn't I know about this?" Feeling out of control, she shook a finger, squinting into her mother's aged blue eyes. Sara noticed a few lines had deepened.

Quickly, she spoke. "Mom, I'm sorry for the way I spoke. It was out of turn, please forgive me. I wasn't aware of the plans. You know with being sick I was not able to come home and help. It's taken a toll on me. I was helpless. I prayed for strength." Tears repeatedly ran down her face.

Louise crossed the room and embraced her daughter, squeezing tightly. "It's okay, I understand. We all say things too sharp and out of turn—sometimes." Louise motioned. "Let me show you where his remains are sitting."

They walked hand in hand into the spare bedroom.

"See sitting on the white bookcase third shelf, he's in the wooden box," Louise said.

Sara swallowed. "Mom, when or where will his ashes be spread?"

Her mom spoke shrilly, "Sara, I'm not sure where or when, but when I do, you'll be notified." Louise turned her back. "That all I want said on the matter at this time."

Reaching the end table, Louise handed Sara her father's Bible. "I have some other things for you of your dad's." She inhaled a ragged breath. "I know he would want you to have them. As you thumb through his Bible, you'll find some interesting things he jotted down about you over the years. Here's a picture of us together. We were photographed for the church directory, less than a week before his passing. I called the photographer and asked if he could crop me from the photo. I explained I wanted a picture of just Paul. He was so nice. He came to the house and had me sign the forms to get permission for the request. He didn't have to come, but he did, and he separated him from the picture."

Sara watched her mom stretched on her tiptoes, touching the top of the refrigerator. Louise ended up getting a chair and handed Sara three pictures of Paul. "Here's one for yourself, and keep one each for the boys."

"Thanks," was all Sara could croak. She found herself laughing and crying at the same time. "Look, Mom. Ah, he's wearing his gray pin-striped suit, just like he wore in Ken's and my wedding.

Look, his dark-brown eyes are not displaying pain. What a blessing. This is a great picture of dad." She clutched it to her chest. "Thank you."

Louise patted Sara's shoulder. "You favored him so through your eyes and his leanness." She touched Sara's cheek. "Why don't you spend the night here with just me?"

Sara glanced at the kitchen clock. "Look at the time. I know Karen and Jud will be all right with the boys, but I should give them a call."

Sara heard Jud answer. "Jud, this is Sara."

"You all right?" Jud asked.

"Better now, thank you. Do you think it would be okay for the boys to stay there for the night? I needed more time with Mother. Does Karen need the car tonight? If not, I can be there first thing in the morning."

"Wait just a moment. I'll check."

Sara heard him called out to Karen, "Sara wants to stay at her mom's. Do you need the car, and is it all right to leave the boys?"

Sara chuckled as she heard the reply, "Heavens, no. We can handle this."

Jud came back on the line. "Sara, everything is fine, and we will call if there's a need. Tell your mother we said hello."

It was midmorning when Sara arrived at the bed-and-breakfast. She was expecting to see her boys with Luke and Luci, but instead, she found a note pinned on the corkboard behind the phone.

It read, "Sara, we took the kids and went to the park. We had extra car seats, so don't worry. I thought you might like some downtime. Your luggage is in room 2B, second floor. The boys' room adjoins yours if the side pocket door is open. Their room number is 2C. You can see each room comes with its own four-piece bathroom. When we get back, hopefully we can talk. Oh, don't forget your meeting at the bank. Your appointment with Jud is at 1:30 p.m. Don't be late. You can use the station wagon instead of taking the bus. Only if you want to."

Sara stretched. "House it's just you and me." She wandered through the downstairs and remarked, "I couldn't have designed this better myself." She admired the old charm of stucco paint over the heavy plastered walls. She appreciated the way Karen had preserved the house and brought back life adding on a second floor.

Sara saw value at the way the front room had been shifted more to the right. It allowed people who entered the front door to step into a sitting area, much like a parlor. She turned slightly to the left, and there was an office. To the extreme left, a stairway opened to a wide-wing stairwell.

Sara thought, *What a rustic sight.*

The wood used, Sara recalled, was from a recycled old fence. She was amazed, and stood there openmouthed. Her fingers trailed on the shiny poplar banister. Standing on the second floor, she did a panoramic view. The doors numbers were etched in Victorian script. The colors seemed understated but quaint. She counted a total of six rooms, or suites, for guests to reside in.

She was surprised when she spotted a secluded second grand staircase. Its twists and turns led her back to the kitchen. She quickly jaunted down the stairs. At the right was a private elevator leading to a third floor. Curiosity got the best of her as she reached for the buzzer. She stood tapping her foot while waiting for the elevator door to open. She heard the ding. She was ready to step forward when she was greeted by Kate Page, and gasped.

"Hello, Sara. I'm terribly sorry for your loss." Kate reached her hand to Sara's arm. "Your father was a good and godly man. We will surely miss him."

Sara bit her lower lip. "Thank you."

Kate cleared her throat. "I saw your boys earlier."

Sara smiled. "Were they being good?"

Kate shifted her purse. "Yes. They are quite cute, and that red curly hair of Matthew's."

Sara giggled. "Matthew's hair color was sure a surprise. I'm sorry, Kate, you must have been on your way out.

"I am."

"Where does the elevator lead to?" Sara asked.

"It's to an apartment," Kate answered. "Karen had it built for her father and myself to live in when we are in town. We've been traveling a lot. You'll welcome to come up and take a look when we both are not so busy."

Sara nodded. "Thanks, I will. Oh my word, look at the time. I have a meeting with Jud in less than one hour and a half. See you, Kate."

Sara hurried to her room and stopped. The ceiling caught her attention. They were at least eleven feet high. She mentally listed her room having a stone inlay fireplace, a razor rolled-back desk, and two golden velvet wing back chairs, which surrounded a quaint round table. She broke into a smile as she noticed a touch of modernism of two floating shelves that had been added on either side of the bed. They each held a tea-light lamp on them.

The overhead ceiling hung an antique fan holding four drip-like candles from the ceiling. Sara walked and used the matching step stool needed to reach the highly polished poster bed. She ran her hand over the quilt. It was decorated in an old-fashioned wedding ring pattern. Sara admired the splashes of blue through-out the quilt piece.

With hands folded, she thought, *What a superb design and high-quality decor Karen formed at this wonderful bed-and-break-fast place.*

She bowed her head and gave thanks for the way He reu-nited friends and how wonderful Karen's dream for the bed-and-breakfast was captured.

Sara rushed as she pulled the green station wagon into the bank's parking lot. It was a chore.

The steering wheel did not want to turn left, and it stayed stiff from not having any power steering. She straddled two spaces. She tried to repark, but it was to no avail. Puffing, she said, "It's sure hard to operate this bomber."

Before Sara opened the car door, she took inventory of herself. She felt for the flower on the left of her hat to make sure it was lodged correctly. She placed her matching gloves on and buttoned only the left one. Satisfied with her looks, she slithered from the car, straightening her yellow skirt.

The walk to the bank caused a lump to collect in her throat. Sara passed through the masculine wood-and-brass door as she headed for the administrator's desk. She removed her right glove to sign in when a way-too-conservative gray-haired woman covered her hand. Her lips were thin. "I'm Ms. Phyler. State your business, young lady."

Sara swallowed. She felt like she had just been summoned to the principal's office. "I'm here to see Mr. Judwin Day."

"Let me check."

Sara watched as the assured lady lifted her hand to knock on Jud's door. It slowly opened, and a nod was given to Ms. Phyler. She walked back, tapping her foot in her high-top laced shoe. It made a clicking as Ms. Phyler reached Sara.

"Mr. Judwin Day will see you, and he will be right out. Now please be seated." She indicated to Sara with a flick of her wrinkly index finger and signed her in.

Sara heard the cherry door open and saw Jud had a wicked smile as he walked over to Ms. Phyler. Without a word, he picked her up and swung her around. Sara giggled and was amused as she watched.

Their eyes locked. There came the finger shaking, and her voice was shrill. "Lady, your father would be so disappointed in you. He would not stand for this nonsensical attitude from you." She fingered her graying hair back and smoothed her bun. She straightened the gold-rimmed glasses on her nose.

Jud tried to look hurt, but his dimple gave him away. "Ah, Ms. Phyler, you know you need to relax a little."

Sara noticed Ms. Phyler had a speck of a smile turning up at the corners of her mouth while she continued. "Now, Jud, you have a visitor, a Mrs. News."

Jud sobered up and turned his attention to Sara. His sea-green-eyed expression changed. He appeared all businesslike. "Hello, Sara. Let me walk you to my office. Mr. Spencer, our attorney, will be joining us soon." He held out a chair for her to sit. "Sara, would you like a cup of coffee?" He was already pouring her one. "Cream and sugar?"

She nodded and shuttered. She would have preferred hot tea.

Jud handed her a cup while he sipped on his.

Mr. Spencer had slipped in and was opening his briefcase.

"Here's coffee, and it's hot." Jud moved and took a chair.

Ms. Phyler stood in the doorway. She cleared her throat. "Want me to take notes, sir? Or do you need anything?"

Jud, glaring, rose to his feet in acknowledgment of Ms. Phyler's presence. He shook his head and, with a dismissive smile, assured Ms. Phyler, saying, "We have everything under control." He took another step. "Ms. Phyler, I don't want us to be disturbed under any circumstance."

Ms. Phyler backed out to the door, and Sara heard the chamber door shut.

Sara watched as Jud turned in her direction.

3

Jud stood and introduced Sara to the attorney then took a seat. "Will you explain the nature of your business to both Mr. Spencer and me?"

Raking her tongue across her lips, Sara cleared her throat. "I first want to thank you both for allowing me to schedule an appointment with you."

Jud scooted his chair closer and placed his empty cup on the table.

Mr. Spencer waved a forefinger. "Sara," he said gravelly. "What do you want to do with your proposed business, and where do you see its growth?"

Sara opened a cloth bag and pulled out worksheets in triplicates. She passed one to Mr. Spencer and then to Jud, keeping a copy for herself. She cleared her throat. "If you will take a moment to examine, you will see I have an itemized list from thread, buttons, zippers, needles, materials, and thimbles budgeted for my project. I also targeted a room for future building set aside in the budget for an office and a workshop."

Mr. Spencer raised a hand. "Sara, you've submitted a completed plan. I'm most impressed."

Jud spoke up. "Before we talk about a contract, I still have a few unanswered questions. First, how does the party plan work? Second, what are you using for a trademark?" Tapping his pencil.

"Third, how do others become recruits, and last, how do they get paid?"

Sara wanted to stretch but held back. Morning had passed well into the afternoon. Her stomach began to rumble. She hoped it would stay silent. Sara heard the door squeak. There stood Ms. Phyler. She gave a light tap at the doorway and paraded in with a table of food and beverages.

Sara smiled. She knew Ms. Phyler couldn't help herself. She was like a four-star general in the service, always looking out for her men. She was a loyal and most faithful employee. Sara noted Jud had been blessed to keep her around when he took over as CPO of his father's bank. Sara knew most of the older employees had retired, but not Ms. Phyler.

Jud unfolded from his chair, giving a nod and brief smile to Ms. Phyler. He quickly motioned midair for her to leave once again, only quietly thanking her this time as she departed. Once again, the door echoed.

Sara blotted her mouth and folded her hands until the men were through eating. After the break, Sara answered the questions, and Mr. Spencer explained any raised thought Jud had expressed. Sara was glad to see both gentlemen nod and have a smile on their faces.

Jud stood. "Sara, let's do it. Let's make this business happen."

Mr. Spencer spread the papers and showed Sara where to sign.

She had butterflies in her stomach but plunged forward. She signed and shook hands with the attorney and with Jud. Sara had to laugh as they stacked their hands on top of each other as if it were to really cinch the deal.

Totally a man's thing, she thought.

"Sara, I trust this adventure will gross many sales, making us all prosperous," Jud stated. "Thanks for coming so well prepared. All the facts were surely there to back you."

Sara could feel herself turn pink. She willed down her blushing and neatly filed the paperwork of her signed contract in her carpetbag. She shook hands again with Jud and fixed herself before walking from the office. She smiled and nodded to the elderly woman as she exited the bank.

Sara felt like she was floating on air as she walked to the car. She thought she would explode. She hurried and shut the car door.

"I did it. I'm now a legal businesswoman." Sara bowed her head. *Thank You, for You're in everything.*

Sara hit the steering wheel. She was excited. She needed to tell Karen and call Ken. She stared the engine, and it sputtered and coughed, and again, a cloud of black smoke appeared then it purred.

Sara didn't know how she had gotten to Karen's driving, for she was caught up in her new adventure. She high-stepped into Karen's office and used the phone. She placed it on speaker as she reached for her papers. "Hello, this is Sara. May I speak with Ken?"

"Hello, Sara, this is his assistant, J. J. Your husband is out. I don't know when he is returning. I'll let him know you called should he come in."

Sara tapped the phone. "Hello, hello?" But the line was dead except for a *buzz, buzz, buzz.* She placed a hand on her hip. "If that doesn't beat all. J. J. disconnected us." She was still looking at the phone, having trouble placing it on the receiver. She shook her head. "He had hung up—on her."

The smell wavered through the air. Karen was fixing dinner.

"Sara, is that you, and if so, can you help out?" Karen called out.

"Sure." Sara reached for an apron. "What would you like me to do?"

Karen looked over her shoulder. "Set the dinner table for us, please. Let's see, we will need four adult plates and four kids' place settings. I would also like to have an extra sitting to welcome company if any should stop in."

Sara smiled as Karen banged pots and pans. She had flour all over the kitchen counter and floor. Sara signaled as she checked the baked chicken. She noticed Karen had used ground cornflakes as the batter. She looked up. "Karen, it needs about thirty-five minutes longer."

"Okay," Karen said. "I'll start the gravy. Can you reach me the big iron skillet?"

Sara shook her head at the way Karen could make an awesome meal out of nearly nothing. The potatoes were boiling, and soon, they would be mashed. Fresh green beans were steaming in their casserole dish with pieces of bacon sprinkled across the top.

Sara, upon instruction, opened the refrigerator door and took out the freshly tossed salad and Karen's specialty brewed ice tea, placing them on the table. Sara thought she could tell Karen her good news after dinner.

Sara was amused with the beveled glass dinner bell Karen still used. As it jingled, you could hear scampering of feet headed to the table. All stood behind their appointed chair and held hands, and a prayer of blessing was given.

Small chitchat was offered during the meal. Sara saw all plates were cleaned. Karen carried the hot peach cobbler and motioned for Sara to get the ice cream. Both were headed to the table when the front doorbell chimed. Jud unfolded himself from the chair, placing his napkin there, staking his claim, and headed toward the door.

It was Ken.

Jud placed an arm around Ken. "Glad you could make it."

Sara saw Jud and heard familiar voices.

"Hi, Sara." Ken turned to Karen. "Am I in time to eat?" He showed an impish smile.

Karen smiled. "There's a place next to Sara. Take a seat."

Ken gave Sara a brief kiss and turned to the boys and Luci. "Hi, Timmy, Matthew, Luke, and Luci." He didn't expect an answer, so he bowed his head and then dug in.

Sara's mouth gaped open, and her eyes widened. "What are you doing here, Ken?"

In between bites, he nodded toward Jud. "He called and informed me about your loan going through. He also told me how impressed Mr. Spencer was with your charts and demon-stration." He took another bite. "You were not only prepared, but you were very well organized." He laid down his fork and, lifting his arms in the air, stretched.

Sara felt heat begin at her neck and continue to her face. "Ken, it's your organizational skill that helped me to be prepared." She reached and kissed his check.

There was clapping all around the table. Karen got up and gave Sara a big hug. "We have to talk."

Ken asked, "Is the pool still open?"

Sara saw Karen's hopeless plea before she answered, "Yes, it is."

"Mommy, Mommy." Different voices to different moms were calling.

"Sara, borrow one of Karen's swimsuits, and join Jud and I," Karen ordered.

Sara looked a Karen. "You come also. I'll help with the kids." Hunching her shoulders, she answered, "Guys, we'll meet you at the pool in forty-five minutes or less."

Sara was amazed as Luci nudged Luke to help her clear the table. Timmy joined in while Mathew sat and watched.

Jud motioned to Ken before they went upstairs. "Ken, come out-side to the front porch."

"What's up, Jud?" Ken asked.

Jud raised his arms. "Ken, I'm working on a program to be placed on a disk for your computer so Sara's sales will be easier to keep track and read. It will also allow her to keep a record of the progress of those she hires."

"Jud, sounds like this program is the way of the future. And by the way, friend, thanks for helping Sara."

"She earned the loan on her own merits."

Both men indicated agreement and shook hands with understanding.

Jud placed a hand on Ken's shoulder. "We better get to the pool, or our names will be mud."

Ken broke into laughter as Jud followed behind.

Karen slipped her big toe into the springwater first. "Sara, it feels wonderful. Nice and warm, yet cool to the touch."

Sara didn't wait. She tucked her knees underneath herself and jumped in. She flittered awhile. "Karen, look, the new salt filter helps me float."

All of a sudden, there was a big splash and then another. It began.

"Do it again!" the twins screamed to Ken and Jud.

Karen took a seat on the steps and let the water surround her. Sara gave up floating and turned to watch. Ken caught Luci and threw her over his shoulder. Jud tossed Timmy to Ken, and over the shoulder he went. They went through all the kids until Timmy, Luke, and Matthew called to Luci and they decided to play with the beach ball.

Karen beamed, for the men had worn the kids down. Jud looked at Karen as the time had passed, and winked. Karen stood walking with Jud, and he paused, taking her hand. "Ken, Sara, the day tribe will see you tomorrow. It's time to get the kids ready for bed. Night, all."

Karen blew her friends a kiss. "You want me to take the boys?"

Before there was an answer, Timmy, holding hands with Matthew, stood beside Karen.

"Will you read to us, please?"

Karen gave a thumbs-up and looked at Sara. She took the boys' hands, leaving Sara and Ken to themselves.

Jud saw that Luke, Timmy, and Matthew showered, while Karen gave Luci a bubble bath. Karen went to the adjoined reading room by their beds. All sat on the floor, including Jud, as she magically carried them away. She saw mouths yawning, and she had to cover hers not to gap. The twins each were tucked in bed in their rooms, and then it was the boys' turn.

Karen wrapped her arm around Jud's waist as they walked to their room. The lights were low, and she leaned into him, placing a hand to his chest. He let out a breath. She stood on her tiptoes and kissed his cheek. He embraced her. "Karen, come lay with me."

Sara returned to floating. Ken swam up beside her, stopping long enough to create a splash. Startled, she gasped, splashing her hands and feet. She was not being successful as he reached for her shoulders and pulled her up. His large eyes had smile flecks. They swam with her on his back, then side by side, as they frolicked in the water. He still caused a stirring deep within her as he planted a kiss on her lips. She felt herself quake.

Ken winked and fingered her back. She batted her lashes and slid her hand into his hair. She pulled his ponytail and bit her lip when she saw the wicked look he gave right before he pulled her close and lightly touched her lips. She slowly pulled away. "Let's go, Ken." She gave him a towel, and she slipped into her robe. Together they climbed the stairs. She turned on the shower and looked over her shoulder.

She mouthed, "I won't be long."

The next morning, Karen and Jud checked on the kids. They were like bugs in a rug, sleeping arm-in-arm. Karen looked at Jud. "Wish you could be here today."

He slowly spoke with uplifted lips. "I am. I called work and had Ms. Phyler rearrange my schedule, but she could handle business."

"Wonderful." Karen clapped. "We are going on a picnic. I was up earlier and made peanut butter and jelly sandwiches, cleaned fruit, baked soft cookies, and made tea to take."

"Can Ken come?"

"Sure. I have enough food."

Sara overheard about the picnic while walking into the kitchen. "Need any help?"

"Let's make a few more sandwiches to be sure." Karen said.

"I'm on it."

"Thanks, Sara."

Karen breathed. *Watch over all of us, and thank You for our time together.*

Humming, Karen closed the lid on the picnic basket. "All aboard. Who wants to ride in the green bomber?"

Everyone lined up beside her car.

"Funny, funny, guys." Kate whined.

"Mom?" Karen twisted her head as she saw her mother.

Kate had popped in from nowhere. "I see a picnic is in store. Beautiful day. The clouds have ducks, sheep, and look, a waterfall. I can also drive."

"Mommy, I don't see anything in the sky except the sun." Luke said.

They giggled, and Karen touched Luke's head and said, "Are we going?"

Karen and Sara were helping the four kids get in when Louise said, "Wait for me. I'm going. It looks like fun."

Karen looked at her mom. "You're driving?"

Kate motioned for Jud and Ken to come as Louise settled into the car. She waved to Karen with her white hankie. "I'll follow you."

An hour later, they were at the park. The children jumped out the car, cheering.

Karen looked at Sara and Jud. "They're running wild, Jud. Let's play a game."

"What?" Jud asked.

"Flag football, of course."

"Got any cloth for tails?"

The boys *eeed!* and clapped their hands. Ken joined in with Jud.

Louise said, "Here's some material for the needed tails."

Karen was amused as she looked toward the blanket and saw a sewing basket and reading books lying there.

"Mom," Luci said with fisted hands on her narrow hips. "Do I have to?"

Karen nodded and passed out scraps of material to be used for the tails. Sara helped her poke the children's tails into their back pocket.

Karen handed Sara hers, and she poked the tail into her bow tie at the back of her dress.

Kate touched Karen's hand. "Sweetie, Louise and I will set this one out. We will try to keep score," she said, laughing at the lineup.

Louise blew the whistle, and they were off. Luci got Ken out first. He gasped. "Karen, I didn't see her coming." Ken trotted over and sat down with Louise and Kate, shaking his head.

The whistle blew again.

Timmy darted to Karen and grabbed the tail. He slid into her, and they both went down.

Kate whooped. "Wow, Timmy, you all right? Help Karen up. Thank you."

Karen pretended to limp off but couldn't keep a straight face.

The whistle blew.

Sara grabbed Luci's tail. Jud got Sara's, and just as Timmy pulled Jud's tail, Matthew had Timmy's tail. Matthew jumped and squealed.

Kate and Louise stood and announced, "Matthew, you're the winner."

Everyone clapped.

The wind was mild and the sun was bright, but it felt tolerable. Karen asked Sara to help as she lined the children up to get a drink at the park's water fountain.

Kate clapped and said, "Hurry, it's time to play Red Rover, Red Rover, Send Someone Right Over."

They played for an hour, and then they were ready to eat.

Karen reached inside the basket and handed each person a well-wrapped peanut butter and jelly sandwich, a piece of fruit, a cookie, and a cup of tea. Karen laughed when Jud and Ken held up two fingers and had a boyish expression on their faces as they reached for seconds.

Louise opened another blanket so they could all sit and spread out. Jud wiped Matthew's hands and face. He wandered over to the Louise and sat down. He toppled over and stayed asleep.

Karen went to sit beside him. She touched his brow with a gentle kiss.

Jud touched Karen shoulder, whispering, "Ken and I are taking Luci, Luke, and Timmy for a stroll. From there, we will go feed the ducks. Maybe you and Sara will get caught up on everything."

Karen squeezed his hand and kissed his knuckles.

Sara seized the opportunity, and explained to Karen, Kate, and her mother about the new business adventure. Clearing her throat, she said, "Karen, will you be a hostess for my first purse show?"

Kate spoke up, "Oh, she would love to."

Karen smiled and shook her head.

Louise, Kate, and Karen started talking all at the same time, naming guests who are to attend the purse party.

Sara observed Karen's and both mothers' chitchat. She tilted her head backward, tittering at all their planning. How could she not be a success?

4

The pond had a lot of cattails surrounding the outer edges. The ducks were lined up around the water, squawking away. There were mallards and woodlands swimming. There were even a few white ducks someone most likely had dropped off from an Easter present. Although they were away from their natural home, they darted into the water.

Timmy was instructed to stand at the grassy spot where he been shown, but he couldn't quite stretch his arm to reach the water. He tested the ground's firmness and stepped closer. In his excitement, the ducks swam closer, nibbling to get his bread feeding. He laughed with glee, moving another step. The ground had softened in spots, and gave way beneath his feet.

Jud unfolded himself and poked Ken. They were only a couple of feet from Timmy. "Something doesn't look right, Ken."

Ken turned with Jud and looked. They discovered Timmy was fading from sight. Just then Timmy yelled "Help!" at a very high pitch. The ducks hadn't moved, and they bobbed, grabbing the food out of his hand before swimming off.

Luci started jumping up and down, crying. "Help him, Daddy."

Luke, being an inveterate swimmer, darted between his dad and Ken, offering to help Timmy. Luke sprawled out on his belly and stretched out his hand. Jud heard Sara leaping. He turned and saw her leap like a deer.

"I see him." It was all she muttered.

"Dad, he's too far out in the pond."

Jud quietly reached for Timmy, but he bobbed out of reach. Sara threw her rubber carpetbag to Ken, and he tossed it to Jud. Ken quickly instructed Luci to stay with Matthew. Jud, in the meantime, stretched his lengthy frame and hollered to Timmy, "Grasp hold of the purse!"

Timmy started flapping. His little fingers just touched the purse. Jud wormed and was able to catch Timmy's shoulder. Ken had sat on Jud's feet, trying to keep him on the ground and anchored. Jud pulled Timmy in and lifted him out of the water.

Luci pointed to Matthew. She ran, and almost knocked Timmy over. She held him in her arms and placed many kisses on his cheek. Both were soaking wet.

Sara hurried to huddle with them. "Timmy, are you all right?"

He shrugged her off with a little shiver. "What's the big deal, Mom? Jud and Dad were here, and besides them, my bestest friend ever, Luke."

"I want to hold you and shake you all at the same time," Sara scolded. But holding him was what she did.

The boys, with Luke and Luci, walked with Jud as Sara walked with Ken. He announced, "Picnic is over. Time for getting back to Karen's house. Showers are much needed."

The women, Kate, and Louise gathered the blankets, the sewing kit, and the books. At the same time, the ladies shouted, "We're ready to leave!"

Karen reached for the picnic basket and edged over by Sara. She still was clutching her chest. *Thanks for Your help.*

Karen leaned in. "Sara, He's here, and He cares."

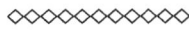

Donald came home, calling out for Kate, but instead found a note. It stated, "We went on a picnic. See you later. Love, Kate.

PS: Would you please start a fire in the parlor's fireplace? Thanks, Donald."

Within a half hour, the group walked through the door and heard the fire crackle. Its roaring kindled and felt good. Karen, Louise, Kate, and Sara held out their hands and Kate remarked, "The warmth seems to touch your bones. It sure takes the chill out of the air and the dampness away."

Karen turned, hugged, and thanked her dad for his thoughtfulness in building the fire.

Donald hunched his shoulders. "The fire was all Kate's idea." He winked. "I read the note."

The children returned from their bath or shower. Timmy pulled on his grandma's skirt. "Can I spend the night with you?"

Matthew cried out, "Me too, Grandma!"

Luke spoke up. "Can Luci and I come?"

Louise placed her arms outward, enticing them to come nearer. She raised a hand to Sara, Ken, Jud, and Karen. "I think I can accommodate all the children very nicely in that big house. Let's pack an overnight bag and go get some cookies and milk."

Karen tried to refuse her offer, but Louise scrunched her nose. Karen bit her bottom lip to remain silent.

Jud nudged Ken. "Help me switch the car seats then ride with me. Then we can drop off Louise and the kids at her your house."

"Okay," Louise said.

Ken nodded and carried his shoes out the door. "Karen, would you brew a pot of tea for us? I'll grab a snack."

Taking a nibble, Sara said, "Karen, it has been good to be here."

Karen poured each a cup of tea, adding only a lump of sugar to hers. After stirring, she lifted the cup and took a sip. Sara followed and carefully sipped hers.

"Your bed-and-breakfast is fabulous," Sara said. "I wouldn't change a thing. It's a great design. The decor is unbelievable."

Karen's smile broadened. "Thanks, Sara." She folded her hands. "Now tell me about, well, you know, Matthew, and then more about your new enterprise."

Karen, amused by Sara's story, said, "I take it Ken liked your little yellow number worn on your anniversary. Hmmm." She began tittering.

"Ken still jokes about the fireworks," Sara joined in heartily.

Karen picked up her cup and sipped some tea. Sara shifted and reached in her bag. She pulled out the plans about her business. She began with a gleam in her eyes and shifted to sit straight.

Karen asked plenty of questions, and Sara willingly answered each one. Sara took another sip then pointed at her charts. She tried to explain how the plan worked. A brief quietness passed.

"Karen, thank you for booking the purse show with me," Sara said. "You'll make out like a bandit. There are a lot of gifts a hostess can select from."

Karen shifted but stayed focus.

"I need you to understand, Karen, there are three styles of purses to choose from. One is called the box. It is square in measurements and made from metal. On top there is a plastic or cloth handle. The next purse is called the envelope. It is an oversized style, shaped just like a legal envelope, only three times the size. This one is made from leather, rubber, or cloth. It has a chain on top by which to carry if one chooses. The third purse is called a sling bag. It's made from burlap or quilt pieces. The bag has a shoulder strap attached to carry the purse over the shoulder."

Karen twirled her fingers. "Would you come into the kitchen? I'll cut us a slice of apple walnut pie."

They ate some pie. Sara placed the fork down and helped Karen cleared the table. She gave the dishes a quick rinse and joined Sara. "My interest in making purses began as a hobby, but folks in Mississippi kept ordering them for different reasons and occasions, so after searching and praying about a business enterprise, I had inner peace and decided to confide with Ken. He gave a thumbs-up and suggested I come to Ohio and work out the business details with Jud through the bank."

Karen drew her chair nearer. "You're amazing, Sara. Don't you think your design degree help?"

Sara blushed a pink hue. "See my samples. Each purse has a little difference to them. They are personalized by a button, snap, or a zipper for closure. People order the style they want, and it is matched closely with their color preference. I also take a supply with me so they can be bought outright.

"Others order from a catalogue, which takes four to six weeks for the person to receive their purchase. All monies are placed up front at the time of their order, which would include tax, handling, and shipping cost.

"My hostess, on a hundred-dollar show, receives one box purse free. On a two–hundred-dollar show, my hostess will receive an envelope purse. On a two-hundred-and-fifty-dollar show and three bookings, the hostess will receive one box or one envelope purse along with a sling purse."

Karen sat spellbound with her mouth gaping.

"See, Karen, why I said you would do so well?" Walking into the kitchen, Kate poured herself a mug of coffee and sat down. "Sara, dear, you have really become an entrepreneur! It can be hard for a woman to have a business, but I have faith in you."

Donald had followed, and stood in the doorway. He walked over to Sara. "Your dad would be so proud of you. He had such a good business head on him. Now I see where you get it. I enjoyed doing business with him throughout the years while he was able." He placed a hand on Sara's shoulder. "He was a good friend."

Sara hung her head and let out a long breath.

Kate touched Sara's hand. "I wrote a list of women I think would come to the party, or least consider being a hostess. Karen, take a look. What do you think?"

Karen fingered the list and quickly added a few more names.

Sara reached into her bag and pulled out the invitations. "Let's get busy, ladies."

Sara looked at Kate and Karen as they were stretching their hands and fingers outward. Karen placed the written invitations in the outgoing mail.

The door opened with a squeak. It was Jud and Ken. As they entered, Jud said, "Hey, Ken, did you bring your guitar?"

Ken motioned to the corner closet. He picked up his guitar and began strumming. Everyone moved into the parlor. A chill wove through the room. Donald put another log on the fire and took a seat next to Kate. Sara gave Ken a wink and scooted next to Karen. Karen clapped with glee as Jud stared strumming. It had been years since she heard him play and sing. He grinned as Ken tuned then began picking. Soon they were playing. Several songs were sung.

Ken and Jud both knew how to draw in their audiences. Being older, the men knew how to charm. Both motioned, beckoning the folks to join with them. Then they would sing without instruments and beat the rhythm out on the guitar.

Sara, Kate, and Karen stared singing and clapping. Donald got caught up in the moment and tapped his foot and bellowed out the song with them. They knew he was off-key, but Kate smiled and patted him on the knee.

The evening time passed by so quickly. Jud and Ken had definitely put on a performance. The music was a wonderful way to end a most interesting and adventurous day.

The men were quite good, and at one time, before marriage, they played in their own band. They were invited for churches, local outings, and at the county fair. Now it was only a passing hobby, and they did not often play.

Donald stood, taking Kate's hand, and excused them from their midst. "Good night." He had a wicked smile as they headed toward their apartment.

Karen looked at her friends with a twinkle in her eyes. "Tomorrow comes early around here, so I'm turning in also." She did an overemphasis in a yawn. "We'll talk more about the purse party tomorrow. I'm so excited."

Looking around, Sara suddenly realized how exhausted she had become. Unfolding from the chair, she took Ken's hand. "Tomorrow it is. Good night, Jud."

Jud stood and nodded. He made haste checking the doors. One could hear banging and light clicking as he took the steps two by two. He quickly had joined Karen. He turned, seeing Ken following Sara still lingering on the stairway.

Jud bent, brushing a strand of hair behind Karen's ear, and lightly touched her cheek with a kiss then whispered, "Our friends seem much in love."

She entwined her hands around his neck, nodded, and yawned again. She stepped away and opened the bedroom door. "I'll get undressed in a moment."

Karen climbed onto the bed. Her eyes became heavy, and her eyelids fluttered. Karen saw Jud reaching for the cover, and as he stepped backward, he whispered, "Karen, you are so beautiful. You still take my breath away."

She attempted a smile, but her eyes fluttered closed.

Jud, being an early riser, had the coffee brewing. The dawn, with rays of pinks, was just cracking through the white puffy clouds.

Ken approached the kitchen, ready for physical labor. "Jud, what's first today?"

Reaching for a mug of black richness, Jud pointed out the window. "See that wood stack? You still have that magical swing, Ken?"

"Let's give it a try." Teasingly, Ken asked, "How about you, Jud? You look a little soft from the last time."

Jud grabbed an ax. "We'll see who's in shape."

The challenge was on.

The wood-cutting chore was completed in no time. Both men stood laughing as Timmy and Luke tumbled out in their PJs. Luke flexed his arm, making a muscle.

Jud knew Luke had years before it really developed, but he made a big issue of how Luke was getting stronger. Ken gave Jud a punch.

Ken said, "Hey, Luke, maybe you can come for a visit. Mississippi isn't that far. Timmy and Matthew would like your help on the ranch."

"Can I, Dad?"

"We'll talk to your mother, but later. Luke, where are you going?" Jud asked.

Karen pecked on the window and motioned them in for breakfast.

As they strolled in, Jud and Ken had a sigh of settlement, looking at the table.

"I'll sit here. Timmy, you sit there." Luke had already sat down and was holding a fork.

Karen wagged her index finger. "Boys, did you forget something?"

Timmy and Luke looked at each other and then to Jud and Ken. Luke laid the fork down, clasped his hands, and nodded with a sheepish grin. "Sorry, Mom."

Jud prayed a blessing, and they dug in. The only noise heard was from the clanking of the silverware.

Luci slowly came downstairs with Matthew. There was a white cloud appearing as they headed into the kitchen. Amused, Jud said, "Matthew, you smell good."

Luci beamed as she held the chair out for Matthew.

The squeak from the floor gave Sara away as she took a seat.

Karen handed her a plate of food and noticed Sara's eyes were still twinkling. She was happy for her friend who had begun a business. It wasn't one of the normal employments or what the expectations were of a working woman. She wiped her hand on the towel and drifted off in her thoughts. She was only too glad to be a hostess for Sara's first show.

Kate entered the room cheerfully. "Good morning."

Donald grabbed a cup of coffee and gave Kate a peck. He tipped his hat to them, and was gone.

Jud and Ken were standing by the sink when the phone rang. Karen, being closer, excused herself. "Hello, KD's Bed-and-Breakfast. This is Karen Day speaking."

"Do you have the Fourth of July this year available?"

"Let me check." Karen realized she had hit the Speaker button as she rustled through the weekly schedule. "How many rooms would you need?"

"We would like to book two rooms having four beds, if possible."

"I can accommodate you. Your names?"

"Brown and Brown of Brown's and Brown Company. Joshua Jimso Brown recommended your place."

"Perfect. How did you wish to pay?"

"Do you take American Express?"

"Sure."

"Okay. Just a minute, please."

The charge machine screeched as Karen side across the form. "Everything went through just fine. Thank you for booking with KD's Bed-and-Breakfast. See you on the Fourth, Mr. Brown and Brown."

Karen glanced into the kitchen, but there wasn't any sign of the men. She heard voices flowing from the parlor as she hung up the phone. She paced herself. Sara and Kate were sitting on the sofa. Karen sat in the old straight-back winged chair and listened as she placed her feet on the large footstool.

Sara pulled out the instruction sheets and passed them out. She wanted to go over the details about the purse parties, leaving no doubt with them.

Kate and Karen nodded. With pen in hand, they got down to serious business about the upcoming event.

5

All the ladies worked hard and had extra chairs arranged in the room. The hall clock ticked seven as the evening hour had finally arrived. It was time for Sara's first purse party.

Excitement was crackling through the air.

Karen patted Jud's arm, and he gave her a squeeze. He paused before leaving. "Karen, Ken and I are taking the four children into Columbus and will view the stores, window displays. We'll also grab a bite to eat while we're in town."

At the door, Jud looked over his shoulder. "You girls have fun tonight."

Ken waved, reaching for Matthew and Timmy, while Jud took Luke's and Luci's hands. Then Ken said, "Good luck tonight, Sara." He winked as they headed out the door.

Karen saw a pink cast rise on Sara's face. She gave a smile and went to the window to catch a glance of the green bomber's taillights disappear in a cloud of smoke trailing off toward the big city.

The doorbell rang.

Karen shook her hands, placing them at her sides. "I'll get it."

People kept arriving in twos, and they followed one right after the other. Sara's stated goal was to have between ten and fifteen ladies attend the purse party.

She moistened her lips for the third time and ran her tongue across her teeth. Sara's eyes widened when she saw twenty-five women seated, and their eyes were all watching her.

Sara had requested Louise and Kate to played door hostess, and to pass out a safety pin with each order form and a pencil to each lady as she came inside. Sara nodded to Karen to bring in the finger sandwiches for the guests, along with her famous brewed ice tea. Everything appeared to be flowing.

Sara took to the edge of the room and began softly, but soon shook off her fears.

The ladies were soon asking, "How long after our order does it take until the purses arrive?" Then different ones stated, "I'll book a show."

Sara gave the clue to Karen, Kate, and her mother to assist helping in taking the purse orders. Sara wanted everything to run smoothly and in a timely manner. Sara looked around and, in disbelief, saw all her sample purses had also been sold.

Throughout the show, the women played a most familiar party game called Pin. Ms. Phyler, of course, won. Her smile broadened. Sara was amused, seeing what a good time old Ms. Phyler from the bank had. She, along with the others, seemed to enjoy the party.

Sara, Karen, Louise, and Kate formed a line to thank the ladies and say their farewells as the ladies exit to their rides.

Sara took her place to add up the show as Karen picked up the trays and beverage glasses. Kate and Louise sat on chairs and pulled them closer to Sara, anticipating what Karen's sales were and what she was going to receive for the show.

Sara nodded and patted a chair for Karen as she entered the room. Karen clasped her hands.

"Karen, you have enough orders and bookings for three shows," Sara said. "The choice is yours, of course, but you have enough in sales to pay for a kit and then some." Flapping her hands outward, she continued, "These bookings would all be yours, Karen, and you would receive payment for doing them."

Sara sucked in a breath. "Karen, you would be in business with me!" She spoke with excitement and clasped her hands while standing.

Karen could only sit with her mouth gaping.

Kate stood and walked toward Karen. "This could be a good thing for you to explore and consider during the bed-and-breakfast's slow seasons." She quickly added, "And you would be helping Sara."

Louise chirped in by seconding the motion.

"Karen, you will be my first recruit," Sara said. "What an adventure this is proving to be."

Karen raised a hand, stopping everyone. She unfolded from the chair with brows in a straight line. "Everyone, give me a moment. Please?" She stepped from the room and raised her eyes upward. *Here I am again. What to do? Help me! Give me peace and the correct answer for Sara.*

Ken, Jud, and the kids came bustling through the kitchen door. Everyone was talking a mile a minute about downtown seeing the lights and all the window displays. The children were excited about where they went to eat. It turned out to be at the city's main hotel. It was their first time. They went on about the chandeliers and linen tablecloths, how the meal was served in three courses, and that Matthew drank the water from the finger bowl. Luke, Timmy, and Luci begin to giggle again.

Kate and Louise shook their heads and clapped. "Come on, kids, let's get you ready for bed. We have another surprise for you."

"What?" the kids said in unison while bouncing up and down.

"Grandpa is going to read to you."

The scampering of little feet filled the atmosphere as they screeched, "Hurrah!"

Karen felt she was in a fog. She sank deeper into the sofa, hearing but still unable to respond.

Jud approached, stooping beside her. "Karen, let's go to our room."

She held out a hand and offered a thin smile. Gliding up the stairs, Karen touched Jud's arm to stop. "Let's check in on the twins. Dad sure is quite the storyteller. Her smile widened as she glanced up at Jud.

In the quiet of their bedroom, Karen revealed to Jud about the business offer from Sara. Jud returned from the bathroom and smacked Karen on her bottom. "I think it would be fun for you." His eyes were sparkly. "Karen, you would be able to call Sara more."

"Jud, there would be a lot of sewing to do for Sara to get my example purses ahead."

"Honey, you could ask your mom to help while you are getting started. You know she would. She might even go on a show or two with you."

"What about Luke and Luci?"

"Darling, we can work out a schedule. I'll take care of them if you decide to give it a try." Pulling the sheet back, Jud patted the bed. "Come, Karen."

Karen saw the emerald lights flicker in his eyes. She turned the light low, padded from the bathroom, and slid under the sheet. She turned to him, smiling, as she used her index finger to trace his mouth.

The green flecks in his eyes deepened. Jud placed an arm under his head and waited. Karen saw his arm flex.

She brushed his muscle and whispered, "Jud."

The peak of dawn came through the window. Karen found the need to stretch. She reached for Jud, but he had already moved. Just his man's scent mixed with musk floated by.

Blinking her eyes around the room, she saw Jud pulling his shirt down. He caught her stare. "Ken's leaving today. I'm sure going to miss him, but he said Mississippi was calling." He gave Karen a brushed kiss. "Ken mentioned he was dropping Sara and the boys off at the airport and then begin his bumpy journey home in the economy rental car."

Karen hurriedly got dressed and skipped to the kitchen. The morning meal was over, and Karen saw her friends' packed bags. She thought their time together was too short.

There was a sound. Karen glanced at Sara as a chair moved. Sara, with raised eyebrows, entered and had the papers ready for Karen to sign. Karen took a copy after the ink had dried. They hugged. Sorrow and adventure traveled through their eyes, but mostly friendship.

She touched Karen's penny swear necklace, as she did hers. "Karen, I can't wait to get home, but as she shuttered, you know flying scares me. I prayed, and it's still disturbing. My faith doesn't seem to be as much as a mustard seed when my feet are in the air. Karen, my stomach now hurts."

"I know, friend, but He's with us," Karen said. "He promises never to leave you nor forsake you."

They stood in the kitchen. Ken picked up the luggage and carried it to the car. Jud was behind him with the kids' car seats. Timmy and Matthew gave Karen hugs and kisses, and went to hug Luke and Luci one more time.

"Come on, Sara. If we don't hurry soon, you may not be able to leave, for it's iffy when the rains come. They cancel flights assigned if the weather gets too bad."

"Coming." Sara's eyes were red rimmed. A few more tears formed.

Everyone was outside saying their last farewells. Ken, Jud, Karen, Sara, and the kids looked up as they heard gravel. A cab pulled up in front, and the cabbie's hand was stretched forward for his fare as he placed a suitcase down on the driveway.

Louise was holding on to her floppy hat. She placed the suit-case in hand. "Ken, Sara," she yelled. "Wait for me." She shuffled up the drive.

Jud put his arm around Ken. "Let's go back inside."

Ken turned and looked at Sara, raising his brow. "We have ten minutes left here, then we must leave for the airport, or you will miss your flight."

"Mom-Louise," Jud teased. "Why are you running? You're out of breath."

Leaving her hat alone, Louise poked Jud on the shoulder. "Since you asked, I'm going home with Ken, Sara, and the boys." She batted her eyes. "I can't stand not being close to them. I don't have any reason to stay here anymore. Jud, here's my house key. I want you to put my house up for sale. Try and get Mr. Drum for the realtor. Now take care of it, laddy, okay?" She went on speaking. "Jud, you can forward all my information to Ken, and don't dillydally." She poked him once more.

Jud pulled on Louise's apron. "Are you traveling with this on?"

Louise snorted. "Lands no, Jud."

Everyone tried to muffle a laugh.

Ken looked at Sara. She had hunched her shoulders, and was smiling. Ken's eyebrows were pitched. "Not everyone is going to fit in this tiny car."

Karen rushed in. "I'll drive Sara and the boys to the airport. Why don't you take Louise and go on ahead?"

Louise interrupted, "Stop, no! Thank you, Karen, but the boys and I will ride with their father. You go on ahead and take Sara to catch the plane. I'm going to get more acquainted with my grandsons Timmy and Matthew."

It was Ken's turn to shrug. He reached over to Sara and gave her a peck. Ken's eyes glinted, and the corners of his mouth turned up. "I love you. Guess we'll see you at the house. I should be there in a few days." He shook his head. "Traveling with the boys and your mother will be slower. We most likely will stay a night or two at a motel."

The boys were buckled in, and waved as Sara kissed Ken and her mother. She said. "See you soon. Be careful, and have fun."

Sara backed from the car. She hugged Luke, Luci, and Jud before getting into the green bomber.

Karen jerked into park and hurried with Sara into the airport. They arrived at the gate, and Sara had to run to board.

"Call me after you land," Karen said. "I love you, and I will be praying."

Sara turned quickly, air-hugging her friend one last time, and scurried off, carrying a small suitcase in hand on the plane.

After she boarded, Karen glanced at the flight time. "Flight 323 from Columbus to Mississippi on schedule."

Sara glanced backward for one last look. She saw Karen waving and pointing at her necklace. Sara smiled. She touched her necklace and waved back.

Sara sat in an outside seat, waiting to see who would be sitting next to her. It wasn't long before a stout but toned-looking woman with long red, orange, and yellow hair plopped down.

"Hi." A plump tanned hand stretched forward to shake Sara's hand. "Let me introduce myself. I'm Claudia Bronk from Kentucky." She pushed past, stepping on Sara's toes. She adjusted herself in the seat. "I came to Columbus for a seminar on nursing."

Sara's eyes opened wider as the woman's seat flattened.

"As a certified registered nurse," Claudia continued in a boisterous Southern drawl. "It's a requirement for me to take classes once a year."

Sara understood Claudia had missed the class in her home state, for one of Claudia's horses had gone into early labor.

Sara retrieved her hand. The woman asked, "What's your name?"

Sara rubbed her hands front and back together, forcing the blood to flow. Her hand felt like it had been in a vise grip. Sara opened her mouth to speak.

"What do you do for a living?" Claudia went on. "Are you a mother, housewife, or a schoolteacher?"

Sara fingered her penny swear necklace and cleared her dry throat. "My name is S." She couldn't finish. There was a moment of panic. The airplane experienced an air dip.

Sara froze. Her heart jumped in her throat. Not a word was spoken.

Sara thought, *This ride headed for home seems bumpier than when I flew to Columbus.*

Another air pocket hit, and then another. Sara and the other passengers were tossed forward.

The Gray stewards captured everyone's attention. Pointing, they pulled down an air mask. "Your air mask is right above your head." Next, they gave directions for their usage.

The pilot's voice was heard over the intercom. "It's not calm we're climbing higher. We are experiencing some inconsistency of the weather. The turbulence has played havoc with the number one propeller."

Sara felt her heart beat uncontrollably in her throat. She gasped. She fingered her necklace and prayed. Sweat beaded on the edge of her brow. She wanted to fight the fear, but fear was winning, and the pilot's voice sounded extremely high-pitched.

An unrepentantly crashing thunderous sound zoomed through the plane, shaking it. The pilot's voice was high but stayed steady. "Lightning has hit the transformer, and it's burned out."

Sara peered all around. *What does that mean?* She could hear her heart.

The stewards gave quick, precise directions for crashing. They demonstrated sitting positions and told the passengers, "Breathe in, breathe out, and again, breathe. Please place the oxygen mask now above your head over your nose and mouth."

Sara felt sick. Her stomach rolled, and her head felt light. Sara glanced up, fingering for the mask, but the mask was nowhere in sight. She felt a strong hand on her neck. A mask was shoved over her face.

The voice said, "Breathe."

Sara noticed it was Claudia, as her mind floated.

The plane partly landed in the Ohio River. The pilot had done an outstanding job. Inventory of passengers were taken, and none were found dead. Most had scratches or minor scrapes. A new baby had been born, for it squealed.

Claudia was holding an unknown female woman in her arms. The woman become more aware, and Claudia was glad the ambulances had arrived on the scene. The stewards were gathering information from each person trying to identify each one.

"All the paperwork has been destroyed,"

she, Claudia nervously continued. "Do you know anyone on the plane? Were you traveling with someone or were you alone? What is your first and last name?"

The Stewards followed up with asking for a phone number for them to call a friend, relative, or someone to inform them what had happened to their passengers and let them know everyone was all right. The stewards said the hospital would check each person out as a precaution.

Sara waited, but no one asked her any questions. Instead, she was placed on a stretcher and lifted into an ambulance.

Claudia came aboard and stroked Sara's face. Her voice was loud and rough. "It will be all right. Just relax. Rest."

The flashing lights came on, and what were those screeching sounds?

6

Ken and Louise easily talked with one another along the way. The radio was on low, for it seemed to settle the boys.

They traveled for about three and a half hours, when Louise hit Ken's shoulder and pointed. "I see a motel up ahead." She clasped her hands. "There's a sign stating they serve food. The children need to stretch and play before they rest. I could use a catnap. Couldn't you?"

Ken glanced at Louise. "Let's eat, then I'll play a while with the boys, and you can rest up."

Ken parked and went and got their key. He paid for two extra rollaway beds for the boys and himself to sleep on.

Ken whistled as they walked to the diner. The diner only had soup left, but no one complained. Louise walked to the room while Ken took the boys for a walk. Along the way, they played tag. That led into wrestling until Ken cried, "Uncle."

Timmy and Matthew laughed while they were sitting on top of Ken. Matthew pulled his ponytail, saying, "Giddy up, Daddy."

It appeared almost a normal night, except they were traveling without Sara.

Ken thought, *Life sure had its changes without notice.* Well, well who would have thought Sara's mother would move with them? He looked beyond the first heaven. *Thanks for being with us, and watch over my Sara.*

Ken gathered their things and headed to the room. The boys were soon bathed, and Louise read them a story. Ken found himself enjoying it also.

She explained, "Boys, this story was read to your mother when she was little."

"Daddy, I miss Mommy," Timmy said.

Matthew chimed in, "Me too."

Ken touched their heads. "I miss her too." He stroked his chin and dwelled for a second. This was the first time he and Sara had been apart since they had gotten married. *Wonder how she is doing?*

Ken heard his name, and turned to Louise. He offered the regular-size bed to Louise. He place Timmy beside Matthew. He took the other rollaway bed. The mattress was lumpy, and his feet hung over the edge. The cover was thin and short.

He placed his hands behind his head and counted the pits in the ceiling. Well into the night, he saw the others sleeping. He whispered, "We need Your guidance, strength, and safety. Watch over Sara. Please."

Finally, his lids seem heavy. Sleep floated in.

The morning came, but darkness was all around. Little sprinkles of sun tried to break though the locked bleak clouds. Heaviness held like a weight in the air. Rain threatened its debut.

Louise shivered as she balanced a sack of groceries and two black coffees from the restaurant. She met Ken at the car and placed the food and drinks inside. She helped strap the boys in their seats. Louise checked to make sure everything was packed and put in the trunk.

Finally, she slid in, and Ken took the wheel. She handed Ken a coffee and sipped on hers. She tried the radio stations, but there was only static. Louise placed a hand on Ken's arm. "The boys will sleep until 9:00 a.m. or so."

"I know. They were worn out last night."

"Ken, how do you feel now that I have sprung my coming to live with you and Sara?" Louise held his gaze.

"I'm glad you came with us and that you're staying," he responded. "Strangely enough, I was going to ask Sara if you would like to come live with us and give the South a try."

Louise hit Ken's shoulder as he pretended to be wounded.

At a little after nine in the morning, Timmy spoke up. "Dad, are we almost home?"

"Not yet, Timmy," Ken answered. "It will be a while."

Louise handed Timmy an apple. She pointed to Ken. "There's a fog rolling in. I don't think we'll see much sun today. Is there a road rest around?"

"It's to our right. We must be close." Ken assured.

"There it is," Louise squealed.

The car skidded a little as Ken pulled over at the road rest. Louise looked at him with narrowed eyes.

"Louise, what? We're parked now."

Louise had read the sign and knew there were not any restrooms. "Ken, you want to explain to the boys about the out-doors and where they will be going?"

Ken took the napkins from Louise, scrunching his nose. "Boys, we are going to the restroom where the bears go."

"Black bears or brown?" Timmy asked.

"Neither, Timmy," Ken answered. "It's an expression."

"Timmy, I'm scared," Matthew said. "Where are the bears?"

"Matthew, I don't see any, and I hope we don't, said Timmy. Take my hand." Ken instructed, "We need to hurry and go quietly."

A twig broke, and Matthew began to cry. "Daddy, I don't want to see any bears."

"Boys, people used to say 'Where the bears go' because you use a wooded outside area, for there are not any inside facilities," Ken explained.

Louise had prepared something for them to eat. "Ken, I'm going to see Mrs. Jones."

He glanced her way and nodded. The boys were in their seats when Louise approached. She gained her seat and shut her door. After looking both ways, Ken had the car back on the road.

The wipers whipped back and forth, but there wasn't much moisture. He sprayed window washing fluid, but it only smeared. Only thickness was forming from the rising fog. It was definitely rolling in. Breathing became hard. Windows were shut, and the air defroster was on. The wing windows on the driver's and passengers' side were opened a crack. Nothing was helping.

The closure of the vehicle caused different body smells to peak. Ken's voice was low. "I only can move at a creeping pace. It's slow and slower. The visibility is getting worse."

Ken had to apply the brakes. A log trunk appeared from out of nowhere, and was directly in front of him. They slid again. Ken could feel the heat coming from Louise. He could see her eyes narrowing, and she was mouthing something as she clutched the seat.

Louise turned sideways and began singing. She taught the boys to do rounds of "Row Row Row Your Boat."

Ken took notice. A thin smile was plastered on her face. She was being a real trooper. It had been four strenuous hours of driving. Ken's back muscles ached, and his knuckles were white from straining. He needed to stretch, so he edged the car over. It was a small space, but he maneuvered and parked.

Ken asked Louise to reach for Matthew. She clung onto him for dear life.

Ken advised Louise, "Don't look down, for the roadside is a direct drop."

Louise bit her lip, feeling for a metal rail. It was what would keep them from toppling over. Ken took Timmy, placing him in front, marching single file step by step. Hand in hand, they edged their way to the wall. Ken knew an old path was there.

Ken sighed, as he knew Louise was following. It made the way more treacherous. Ken felt a bump on his back and suddenly stopped. His heart fluttered. It was a flashlight Louise handed him. They began their journey down a steep, bumpy path. They moved slowly and carefully step by step. They couldn't walk far, for the fog was too overpowering and the flashlight became dim.

Ken whispered, "Matthew, Timmy, just squat."

"Don't turn around, Ken," Louise said. "Hold it right there, mister."

Ken heard movement and felt a branch. "Okay. I'm turned. Hand me the boys."

Ken wanted to wait, but this was the only opportunity he had. Ken shuddered. The darkness was so unsettling. Eeriness was all around. Looking but not really seeing.

Watch over us, he pleaded.

They ambled their way back to the car. Matthew stumbled and squealed. Ken's hand automatically flung out, snatching a shirt.

"Stop at the trunk," Louise said. "I have sandwiches."

Ken let out a long breath. "Louise, this peanut butter and crackers are good."

"Just hold the flashlight, Ken. Try using a steady hand."

"Thank you, Grandma."

"All aboard." Ken clapped his hands. "I'm sure glad we're not behind that log truck any longer."

"Me too," Louise said. "You never know, Ken, when fastened logs can come undone. It could take hours for cleanup if there were a spill."

He let out a sigh. "Louise, I hadn't considered a log drop." Gripping the wheel, he glanced at the car's clock. It was bright orange, and showed the time. It was going on 6:30 p.m., and looking at his speed of yet twenty-five miles per hour, Ken spoke softly to Louise. "We'll need to stay somewhere again for the night. It's so hard to see, and the visibility is horrible."

The car moved. He checked, but the column was in park. It wasn't him.

Louise turned, looking at Ken. "What the."

He hunched his shoulders and caught a glimpse outside Louise's window. He wasn't sure, but there appeared to be a huge racked-raggedly-dark-coated something. The car moved again, but this time to the side.

Ken let out short staggered breaths. "Louise, don't be frightened. Just pray. I need you to turn your head very, very slowly at an angle to your right. Don't yell. Please. Don't yell."

"What is that?" Her voice was shrill and piercing. They took another hit, moving the car farther. "What are you going to do, Ken?"

"I'm not sure. First, I'll switch off the headlights, and then I'm stepping on the accelerator slowly. I need to see if whatever it is passes in front of the car. Hang on, Louise. It's coming. I hear its hooves. It's headed for my side this time. Oh no, it's a moose."

Again, nothing could be seen. The sky of blackened purple appeared to gobble up the earth. Ken pulled the headlights back on and pressed the gas pedal for all it had. The moose was still following.

Then a patch of heavy rain fog covered the car, and even being in total darkness, Ken still tried to drive. He made a vow: he never again would get an economy-size car.

It seemed like an eternity passed before they felt safe. Ken let out a long mouthful of air. He was exhausted. He checked the rearview mirror and flashed quickly to the sides. Ken found they had been spared from colliding seriously with the moose. He heard a noise. It was his heartbeat.

Louise's eyes were closed, and her hands folded in her lap. She seemed calm. Maybe she was asleep. He adjusted his hands on the wheel.

"Ken, let's find a place for the night. Okay?"

Startled, his jerk his head. "I'll look."

Mountains were all around them. Louise pinched Ken's arm. Ken quickly rubbed his arm. "Ouch. Geez, Louise."

She punched his shoulder. "There's a neon sign. *Vacancy*."

Ken didn't remember a time he felt more relieved than at the moment. He looked in the rearview mirror, for Timmy had been so silent. Their eyes locked. Timmy clapped as the car made a turn to the left.

The motel sat nearly at the top of a mountain. With a good rain, Ken thought, for sure they would slide down the hill. Hopefully they would be safe and there wouldn't be any mudslide.

There wasn't a place to eat, but the motel's sign advertised a shower. Maybe there would be hot water, and what a blessing that would be.

Ken, not wanting to be selfish, ushered the boys to the sink and washed them off. He gave the shower to Louise. The boys munched on a few crackers Louise had brought in and went right to sleep. Ken slipped off his shoes and stretched out in a chair, crossing his feet out in front of him.

Louise poked him once then twice. "Your turn."

He muttered, "Thanks."

Ken had lost track of time. He felt the kinks ease in his neck as the warmth of the water cascaded down his head, shoulders, and back. He wiggled his fingers, for they were beginning to have some feeling flowing in them. His problem came from gripping the steering wheel. He had been ridiculously tense, and it was as if his actions gave him more control.

He began humming a tune while thinking, *I sure miss Sara. She would have acted more like her mother. She'll get a big laugh at our adventure about the moose when I tell her.*

Ken quickly dried and redressed. He hadn't noticed before, but tonight, Louise was snoring.

Lying there on the cot with hands under his head, he wondered how Sara did on her flight. Drifting, he thought, *I'll see her in just a few hours—about three.*

Sleep invaded.

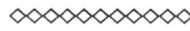

Timmy slammed the trunk close. It was almost daylight. He held his hand out. No fog was left or rain to contend with, only puddles. Everyone climbed in, and they were back on the road traveling. Louise sang. The boys joined in, and so did Ken.

They played, counting the wheat fields, cars, and telephone poles. Finally they were almost home. Only three more roads before turning off. Their dirt road sprayed dust. Louise darted a look at Ken before fanning and placing a hanky over her nose and mouth. They came to a full stop.

"Ken, this is so nice. Look at the porch. I love it. Did you make the chairs?"

"Thank you, and I did carve the chairs," Ken said. "I like sitting out here in the morning and in the evening watching the sun come up and go down. There's a breathtaking view from the porch."

Ken managed the luggage and shoved the front door open. "We're here, Sara. Is anybody home?" He set down the luggage and wandered through the house. "Sara, where are you?" He turned, looking back at Louise. "Everything seems to be in place as when I left it." He raked a hand through his hair. "How can that be?" He shook his head. "Maybe her plane was delayed because of the fog, or she may have stopped off at one of the neighbors' first."

Louise stood in the kitchen, admiring the space. There were lots of cabinets, a huge counter space, and room for a large eating table.

"Welcome home, Louise. Come, I'll show you to your room." Ken picked up her luggage and walked down the long hall. "The bathroom is on the right, and this is your room."

"It's minty, but very attractive," Louise commented.

"Excuse us, Grandma." The boys skirted ahead and went clomping to their rooms.

Ken left Louise after small talk and climbed the stairs to check on his boys. Timmy was playing with his plastic horses and their barn while Matthew was sprawled out on the floor zooming with his toy cars. He backed away, and knew he must call Jud.

After reaching the phone, Ken tapped the receiver a couple of times. He tried placing the call. A message came through: "There's trouble on the line. Try later."

He heard Louise walking. "I can't get through to Jud. There is trouble on the line. I'll try him later." He placed his hands on his hips. "Louise, do you mind if I drive to the bank? I want to see what's been happening since the phone is not working here. Oh, the candles are on the second shelf to the right of the coffeemaker. Hopefully, the lights won't go out. Matches are beside them." Ken gave Louise a hug. "Thanks, and I'll see you soon, I hope. Tell Sara, when she comes, I shouldn't be too long."

Ken shoved out the back door, reaching for a jacket. The wind was whirling. He drove the car to the rental station and turned it in. He hitched a ride to the bank, where his car was parked. He noticed the bank was dark. Why weren't the lights on? He glanced at the window, where a sign hung: "Be back shortly."

A sprinkle hit Ken on the face. He wondered why the bank was closed. The winds started and whipped through his slacks. He grabbed his coat closer.

Just then a man came by. "You open?"

"I will be," Ken answered. "How can I help you?"

"I want to make a deposit before passing through. I had a stop on the other side of town and dropped off a new stallion at a nearby farmer's place. Mr. Hiffs."

The doorbell jingled, and the lights flickered on. They fluttered.

"This way, sir," Ken said. "I'll take care of your deposit. My name is Kenneth News. The CPO here."

The rubber stamp sounded so loud in the empty building as the receipt was marked with the date and the deposited amount. "Thank you for your business and trust. Come again, sir, if you're ever down our way."

The lights flickered again and stayed off.

Frowning, Ken advised the man to be careful.

The humbled man offered, "I heard on the radio that the state of Mississippi is under a severe weather watch. You're probably in for a terrible storm. They say it's coming off the coast of Mexico and headed here."

Ken again thanked him. He watched the man outside zip his coat as he turned to lock the door. In a few quick steps, Ken was in the office. There propped by the phone was a brief note from J. J: "Big storm due to hit. Lines have been down since Tuesday. I sent everyone home in hopes they would be safe. The rains have been iffy, off and on. The lines to our phones and computers are not in service. I left for New York on a visit and will be returning in a couple of weeks. I trust you will find everything in order with the books. Your aide in training, J. J."

Ken found a candle and struck a match. He inspected the books, and nodded. He understood everything was in order. He stored the disk Jud had made in his desk drawer for later so he would install it for Sara.

The window caught his attention as it rattled. Ken looked out. The sky was blackening, and it was wicked looking. Ken left the sign in the window and quickly relocked the door.

7

Ken moved swiftly to the car. The door was nearly pulled from his hand. The wind had really begun its movement.

It was whistling and howling, causing the branches to sway and bend back and forth. The car was being airlifted and blown sideways as Ken was driving. Big marshmallow drops of water hit and splashed on the car's front window. It quickly turned to icy sleet then to ping-pong hail in a matter of moments. Ken's vision became impaired as he strained from any window.

Vehicles had pulled over, for he knew their drivers were not trying to venture any farther in the storm. Gripping the wheel harder, he prayed. *Help your servant.* Instantly, a force stronger than himself drove him, plunging the car homebound.

Even though the winds had whiffed with more speed, the shrillness had begun. The cracking and lightning show caught his breath. Branches were split in two. Some looked like toothpicks. The wind howled. He wiped the front window. There was a form of his driveway—the house barn. Ken took another deep breath and shut off his engine.

He saw the hired hand, Sam, had on knee boots and was holding a lantern, flagging Ken to the barn. The wind whistled and whipped its way around him.

"Ken, your new high jumper is loose. She got spooked with the sounds of the storm and jumped the fence. I tried to stop her, but she didn't look like her feet were even hitting the ground. She's so temperamental." He grabbed his hat and shook his head. "Then I saw this woman headed out here with arms waving in the air. I almost hid."

Ken scratched his chin.

"I know now she's Sara's mom, Louise. She talks fast. A farmer stopped by asking about a horse. He declared the horse was from this farm, and it was now in his field. I waited for you, Ken, it takes two."

"Let's move." Not having time to check with Louise because of the natural elements happening, Ken grabbed his bib overalls, hip boots, raincoat, and hat from the barn. The winds tore at Ken and Sam. Their faces were blistery. They barely could hear each other speak.

Ken's old Ford truck shook and wobbled all the way to his neighbor's farm. Three country miles was a long stretch in weather like this. Ken pointed to the field. Sam hopped out, and Ken was not too far behind. They waded out and put a bridle onto the mare.

Sam used his soothing voice. "Come on, Sugar, you can make it. Let's get you home while the getting is good."

She bolted. Darting a few feet away, she raised on hindquarters, with the front hoofs daring anyone closeness. Her ears tilted backward, and she had become more skittish. One could tell the storm with thunder and lightning was frightening her.

Ken slowly took the rein. He pulled on the horse while Sam pushed. Ken's feet were now stuck in the field. He made a quick discussion and took off his handkerchief and tied it around the mare's head to cover the eyes. Ken jumped on the horse's back. His boots slid off, leaving them in the mud. He muttered, "I'll come back and get them later."

Sam, being lighter in weight, took the bridle and led the way to the truck. It was slow. The rain, sleet, and continuing hail were beating down. The mare moved and stepped into the truck. They got her anchored down. The ride home would be terrifying and slow.

Ken held his head for a moment.

"What's wrong, Ken?" Sam asked.

"My head's throbbing," Ken said. "Not much sleep."

"Want me to drive?"

"No. I need you to look out for the horse."

The truck rocked back and forth like a ship.

The drive home was treacherous. It took over and hour. Ken stopped the truck inside the barn. They pulled, pushed, and shoved until they finally got the mare down and inside a stall. Ken began wiping her down. Sam grabbed a blanket and some oats for her to eat. Sam took over brushing the mare as Ken spread the straw. He added a carrot and some fresh water for her comfort.

Sam had a battery-run music box, and he put an eight-track into it, trying to soothe the horse. "Ken, you head on in the house. I'm going to bunk down in here and stay with her tonight."

All seemed normal again except for the storm. Ken waved to Sam as he headed toward the back porch, mud and all. As he opened the door, the smell of fresh coffee wove under his nose. Ken smiled, and then a shiver ran through him. His whole body started shaking, and his teeth were chattering.

Ken reached for a mug of black coffee that Louise offered. Spilling some, Ken managed a weak sorry and thank-you in between stuttering. "Louise, will you help me get my gear off? I'm all thumbs."

Without hesitation, she nodded and helped stripped off his gear. "Now go. Get in the shower, and make sure the water is as hot as you can stand it. Let me know if you need any boiled."

Ken turned on the shower and adjusted the water. The rain head streamed completely over his body. It became a little balmy, but feeling the warmth come back into himself was enjoyable. After thirty minutes, he reluctantly opened the bathroom door and heard Louise clear her throat. Was she on the steps?

"Yohoo. Ken? Oh, Ken? Donald and Jack are here."

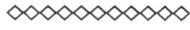

"Hello, ma'am. I'm Dr. Life. You're looking a little more rested today. How are you feeling?"

She stared back in wonder, looking into his wide brown eyes, questioning. "Where's the nurse that was here with me?"

"Claudia?"

She nodded. "She has my clothes. I don't need to be here."

The nearness of his face came closer to her. What was this doctor doing? Strange. In protest, she lifted a hand, making a fist to hit him on his shoulder, but he didn't move. Again she spoke. "Help me sit up. Please!"

Instead, the doctor backed away a step or two and thumbed through a chart.

She eyed through the rails that Nurse Claudia was coming into her room. She would be a great help and fix things.

Claudia placed an arm around the patient's back and lifted her up in bed. She fluffed and placed the pillows behind her head. The nurse offered her a sip of cool water. It just couldn't be refused. She took her temperature and her blood pressure. With wide eyes, she stared at Nurse Claudia. "When am I going home? Can I have something to eat?"

The nurse didn't answer but smiled before she sat down. Claudia opened a magazine and began to read.

Soon, sleep came.

The next morning, she was ready for Nurse Claudia. She held a water glass and spoon in one hand. She was going to pound on the glass, and that would get her attention. She heard her walk.

"Good morning." Claudia looked down. "Here's your breakfast. It's a soft eggs and grits." She placed the tray down and poured some coffee. "I hope you like it black."

Claudia bolstered her up into a sitting position. Sara looked at the nurse with a grave smile. She handed over the glass and spoon in exchange for the food. She picked up the fork and fed her mouth. "This egg and slice of toast is good, but what is that grainy mess?"

She was handed the coffee. She blew then took a sip. She nodded her head in satisfaction.

Claudia waited a few minutes before taking the cup, and then touched her shoulder. "I'll be right back. You try to relax, okay, *Jane?*" The nurse removed the tray and stepped from the room. "Now go ahead, close your eyes."

Her eyes fluttered as she thought, *Maybe we can talk later about going home.*

She yawned, and total blackness came.

It seemed her eyes had just shut, but the room was filled with a streamline of sunshine. It felt warm to her body as she stretched. She pushed and slid downward. She reached for the rails, forcing herself to sit up.

She carefully viewed the room. Where was she? She gasped. It was a hospital, and it looked like she was the patient. She wondered how long had she been there. Tapping her forehead, she recalled Nurse Claudia had called her Jane. Why?

She shrugged and nodded. She decided she wanted to leave. Looking around the room, she saw no clothes. She fixed her eyes toward the hallway while she drummed her fingers on the rail. *Now where is that Claudia?*

Karen recruited her mother in helping her sew the necessary purses needed for the first show. Although still a little stunned, she was also excited. *This could work during the bed-and-breakfast's slow times.*

Two weeks later came the evening for the show. As Karen began, she looked at her mother, catching Kate's square shoulders and her facial smile. Her eyes widened. Kate gave her a wink and folded her hands. Karen readjusted her skirt, smiled, and helped the twenty-five women who came. Her mother helped Karen socialize with everyone.

The hostess party appeared quite successful. Ms. Hersay was excited when she selected two purses she had earned. There were also four shows booked from the party. The congratulations and hugs were given as Karen, with her mother, left.

During the drive home, Karen looked at her mom. "Can you believe it? I made fifty dollars from the show. Thanks for your help."

"How much did you clear after expenses were taken out?"

"Mom, fifty dollars is the amount cleared. The bed-and-breakfast has booked up for the rest of July and most of August. I think things are finally beginning to look up for me financially. You know I want to keep the dowry replenished. There is Luci to consider, for her day will come."

"Yes, Karen," Kate said as she placed her hand over hers. "She'll be grown up before you know it."

Karen went into her office and entered the data from the show. She smiled as she glossed over the program her husband had installed. She reached for the phone to share the news with Sara and to find out how her flight home went.

Looking at the phone, she thought, *Wonder why it just keeps ringing busy. That's probably why Sara hasn't called. I'll ask Jud.*

Jud cleared his throat and stopped in the doorway of her office. He wore that lopsided smile, and had an arm leaning against the door frame. It nearly took her breath away.

"Karen, I hear congratulations are in order for tonight's great show." He swung her around and brushed her lips.

She responded by kissing him. He pulled apart from her, looking wickedly handsome. He patted her arm. "How about coming to bed a little early tonight?"

Her stomach fluttered. She felt her neck heat up and could only nod.

He turned to leave, and Karen could only whisper. "Jud, I tried to reach Sara. Her line rings busy. Have you heard from Ken?"

"No, I haven't heard from him, but it's one of their rainy spells. There was trouble in the lines when I tried earlier. I sent a message to him from the computer, but it didn't go through either. We'll have to wait until they reach us, or unless you choose to write a letter." He laughed. "It might be the fastest way of communication."

Karen stood and walked with Jud into the kitchen. She poured him coffee, and she made ice tea for herself.

"Karen, while Ken was here, he told me he added two new mares on the farm and was thinking about breeding them," Jud said. "Ken thought of maybe moving a little from farming. Oh, one is a thoroughbred and a high jumper."

Karen looked at Jud from the top of her glass. "Sara mentioned that Ken had finished the fencing around the back area of the farm and relieved it was completed before the rains came."

Setting his cup on the counter, he headed out the door but paused. "Ken also said he was building an office with a joined bathroom for Sara. It's to be a surprise. He wanted us to come down for the opening." Jud move outside. "Ken, still the same laid-back person as always." The door closed.

Karen followed Jud to the garage. He was tinkering with a ladder and his mower. "Jud, Sara declared to me how it took her almost a year to settle in Mississippi. She said it took the changing of the four seasons. She thought the land, with its crops of wheat, were like looking at dripping honey, and standing in a distance was breathtaking."

Turning, Jud said, "Ken really enjoys the farm. He said if the rains didn't come the farming would never get done. He laughed when he said it kept him humble."

Karen slid over and gave Jud a pat on the cheek. "You know, Jud, Sara and Ken act more in love with each other than ever. Is that's even possible?"

"Karen, when's your next show?"

"Tomorrow at three. Is that all right?"

"Mmm, sure."

"What would you like for dinner? I'll start before cleaning the guestrooms. Calls have came in, and we're booked."

"Surprise me. Anything you fix is delicious."

She smiled and went into the kitchen. After scouting her supplies, she decided on a chicken vegetable casserole. It was hard to measure just what was needed for the dinner, for her mom and dad had plans out and there would only be the four of them. The mix was done, and the timer was set. She bustled about the kitchen. She brewed tea and placed it on the shelf next to the freshly picked garden salad in the icebox.

Karen climbed the steps, holding the mop bucket and pulling the cart, carrying the supplies to clean with. The twins greeted her. "What have you two been doing?"

"Visiting with Grandma and Grandpa. We had breakfast." Luci smiled.

"Well, your father is in the garage, and I'm sure he could use your help."

Karen was in the hall bathroom backing out from the mopped floor when she shivered. She set the mop down and crossed her arms and vigorously rubbed them. She tried to bring in warmth, but she was stunned. She wasn't cold. Shaking her head, she picked up the pail and mop, slipping to the next bathroom. She completed cleaning all the suites, and when the time had passed into evening, still Karen could not shake off this eerie feeling.

Karen welcomed the casserole. It smelled wonderful. Luke and Luci set the table then carried the garden salad, along with a pitcher of ice tea.

"Come and get it," Karen called. She didn't bother using the bell.

Jud held the seat for Karen. Following his dad's lead, Luke held the chair for Luci. They all held hands. It was Luke's turn to ask the blessing.

Karen scooped the chicken casserole onto their plates and began passing. Next came the salad. Jud passed the bread and butter as he gave Karen a wink. Luci was passing the corn when they heard the phone ring. Jud scooted off his chair, excusing himself to answer the kitchen phone. He hunched his shoulders. "It's probably Ken or Sara." Turning, he lifted the receiver. "Hello. Well, Mr. Nite." He turned toward Karen, covering the mouthpiece. "It's Jack from the study group."

Karen saw Jud arch his brows.

"This is a surprise. How have you been, sir? Karen and I have been meaning to attend your reading group again. Busy, you know." Jud pointed to Karen and mouthed, "Turn on the TV."

"You said RRK's 10 channel flashed a picture of a woman who looks like Sara?" Jud questioned. "The news is over, Jack. We missed it, but we'll watch it tonight. You say the photo is in black and white?"

Karen came and stood beside Jud. She heard the alarm in Jack's voice.

"Have either of you talked with them?" Jack asked.

Karen looked at Jud.

"No, we haven't," Jud answered. "There's been trouble in the line."

"Jud, it's trouble, all right. The weather station stated a rainstorm blew in Mississippi and has brewed there until a 2.5-level wind occurred." Jack cleared his throat. "I've an update from the phone company. They said Mississippi had a mishap with an unexpected storm. Lots of wind and storm damage. A thirty-four-year-old tree, among others, was uprooted. It hit the main transformer, causing a fire, and the transformer blew. There is not any electricity or any open phone lines."

"Jack, I'm sure there is lots of debris that the storm caused," Jud said.

"Well, I didn't mean to alarm you, but the picture on the telly gave off such a remarkable resemblance to Sara," Jack said. "I would like to hear from you. My phone number has changed, though. It is now BR4-3219. Call me, and when you talk with Ken, tell him hello for me."

"I will. Thank you for calling."

"Jud, tell Luke and Luci hello for me. Good night now."

Karen offered to reheat the food, but it looked bland and lumpy. Jud poked at it and scrunched up his nose. "Thanks, but no."

Karen sliced some pie and said, "Here, have a warm piece of cherry pie."

Jud smiled and reached for the coffee. The twins clapped their hands and dug in.

After dinner, Jud went into Karen's office, adding Jack's new number to their directory. Karen, with the twins, cleaned off the table and played a game of checkers. The hour was late, so Karen informed the twins it was bath time.

"Mommy, will you read to us?" Luke inquired.

"Hurry into your jammies."

Luke and Luci clapped their hands at the end of the story, saying, "More, Mommy."

Karen shook her head and ushered them to their own bedrooms, giving them each a kiss. She turned out their light. "Good night. See you tomorrow."

In the hall, she called out, "Love you both."

8

Karen scampered downstairs and fixed a large bowl of popcorn. She met Jud in the living room, where he had turned on the TV station. A commercial was on when Kate came in from hanging up her coat. "What's on?" She turned to Karen and took a handful of popcorn. She walked to the sofa and sat down.

Donald stood beside Jud. "Karen, what smells so good?"

Karen laughed and retrieved another bowl to share their popcorn.

"Jud, what are we watching?"

Another commercial drifted past.

"Donald, Mr. Nite called and spoke about a photo in black and white that was on the news earlier," Jud said. "He thought it resembled Sara. I told him we would watch the news and see if they reflashed the picture."

Karen's index finger was waving and pointing. The four focused on the set. "Look at the screen. It's rolling something. 'Does anyone know this person?'"

All four sat glued to the TV. They were trying to make out the face. It wasn't the best photo of the woman, and then the news switched over to other things.

Jud stood and began pacing with fist at his sides. "What if it was Sara? I can't even reach my friend since the lines are down."

Donald unfolded from the sofa and placed a hand on Jud's shoulder. Karen had her hands in her lap and was slumped over as Kate let out as gasp, covering her mouth. The phone rang again, and Karen jumped.

Jud took the phone. "Hello? Wait just a moment, and I'll put you on speakerphone. All right, Jack, go ahead."

"Jud, did you get a chance to see the photograph?" Jack asked.

"We did, but we are as unsure as you are. I'm going to call the TV station and see if I can get any additional information."

"I already did, Jud. They said a hospital in Kentucky forwarded the picture to them. They stated the woman arrived at their hospital two days ago without any paperwork. The woman doesn't have any recollection as to who she is or where she is from. Isn't it all so mysterious?"

Karen took her mother's hand.

Jud nearly choked. "Well, I need to find away to communicate with Ken."

"Jud, the wires are down in Mississippi for at lease three weeks per the station's report," Jack said. "I would try flying there."

A brief silence occurred.

"I'm book to leave for Brazil tomorrow," Jack spoke. "I've scheduled an interview with a prominent teacher of the poetic arts. I should be back in a week. I'll call you, Jud, and see if you have heard anything."

"Take care, Jack, and good luck," Jud responded. "Call when you can, and I'll see what I can do." He paused. "What's that, Jack?"

"Remember, He cares," Jack said. "Bye for now."

Jud stood holding the receiver. His shoulders went limp, and his breathing appeared shallow. Karen moved to Jud, cuddling him in her arms. Tears fell from both.

Donald stated, "Let's think positive and make a plan."

Kate spoke, "We could call the hospital or TV station."

Karen waved her arms. "Wait. find out if the woman checked in at the hospital was wearing a necklace like mine." She fingered her necklace. "It's called a penny swear necklace. try asking for the hospital administrator."

"This is good we're planning. We're getting somewhere now." Kate said.

New hope began this ongoing of Sara's adventure.

"Hello, my name is Judwin Day," Jud spoke. "I would like to speak with the person in charge, featuring the photo of the missing woman."

"One moment, please."

"Thanks Donald." Jud took the cup of coffee offered to him. "I'm on hold."

Five minutes passed, then ten.

Jud placed his massive hand over the receiver. "They sure are slow."

Donald patted him on the back. "Now, now. Patience has never been one of your strong points, my son."

"You're right, Donald," Jud said. "Ken is the one that's laidback." He turned back to the phone. "Hello? Yes, I'm Mr. Day. I do have a few questions. Would you know if the woman from the hospital featured on your station wore a necklace? It would have looked like a penny."

Slowly a heavily accented answer came. "Couldn't tell you if she did or if she didn't."

"Well, who can give information about the photo of the woman ran on your station?" Jud asked.

Everyone saw Jud pacing and blowing out a breath. Donald tapped him on the shoulder and reached for the phone.

"Sorry." He glanced at Jud and, in the same breath, said, "Hello, my name is Mr. Donald Page. I'm an in-law of the person you were just speaking with. May I please have a moment of your time? Thank you." Donald switched the phone over to speaker once again. "We think this unidentified woman may be a very dear friend of ours."

Jud continued pacing the floor with hands in pockets jiggling change.

Donald stated, "It may help clear up who this woman is. Make it quick." He paused. "Since the photo seen was in black-and-white, do you have a description of her? Like, did the woman in the photo have short curly raven-colored hair? Her height would be about five foot two inches. She would weigh about a hundred and maybe fifteen pounds, and have brown eyes."

A shuffling of papers was heard. "Hello. This is Bob at the station. I'm not sure about the woman, no description was forwarded, but the hospital personnel, Mr. Roberts of Administrations, may be able to talk with you or even see you. Sorry we couldn't be of more help. Good luck. Hope you folks get answers about the woman."

"I'll try calling the hospital, Bob, and see if we can meet with them. Again, thanks for your time. Good-bye, Donald said."

Jud's lips were thin. "Look, Donald, I'm sorry I let my temper get in the way. I almost messed everything up with them." Clasping his hands, he lowered his head. "Forgive me?"

"I understand," Donald said. "Not being able to contact your friend is nerve-racking in itself. It makes you feel helpless."

"Thanks for being understanding and being here for me." Jud stopped. "Donald, there's another problem. I won't be able to travel with you to the hospital in Kentucky."

"Why not, Jud? I can do the talking, if that's your concern."

Jud held his hands up in a plea. "I haven't been able to say anything about this, but I'm scheduled in court over a new ruling that may change the way we do things at the bank." He put his hands through his hair, rubbing the back of his neck.

Donald patted Jud on the back then immediately turned toward Kate. "I need a few things packed for a couple of days."

Kate left the room and did as she had been asked. She pulled out the oversize brown suitcase on wheels and laid slacks, dress shirts, socks, underwear, a sweater and a suit coat just in-case and several ties and remembered to add his shaving articles and Bible. Kate walked down the steps towards Donald.

Donald placed a call to the hospital. "Great, thank you." He faced them. "I have a meeting with Mr. Roberts at the hospital in the morning. Karen, you gather pictures of Sara when she was a teen and a few of how she looks now." He took Jud's hand. "You call Jack and update him. Tell him I need to speak with him as soon as possible. It's urgent."

Donald gave Kate a hug. "I'll call you when I'm settled at the hotel." He looked at the suitcase. "Are the pictures packed?"

"They're on top, Dad, said Karen."

Jud put one arm around Karen, drawing her close as he shook Donald's hand with the other. "Be careful."

A silent look was cast between the men.

"Thank you."

Donald rushed to the airport, parked, and carried his suitcase. He was surprised to catch a Sunday-night flight. He opened his case to view the pictures Karen had sent. He saw an envelope and pulled out a picture of Sara with Karen walking up the homestead driveway hand in hand. One of Sara's pictures was of her at the engagement party. The most recent photo was of Sara wearing the penny swear necklace at Karen's purse show.

Donald notice Karen had even packed a sales report with a note that said, "Call me, my best friend in the whole wide world." He placed a handkerchief to his nose and bent his head. *Hear me, oh Lord, and help us in this our troublesome time.*

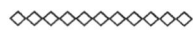

"Hello, Kate," Donald said several hours later. "My flight went smoothly. I've already checked in at the hotel and have placed a wake-up call and a light breakfast for me. Wish Jud good luck in the court for me. I'll call with updates. Love you, Kate. Good-bye."

The phone line buzzed, and he placed the receiver down.

He lifted his Bible and read his evening devotions. Donald pushed his glasses up twice and decided it was time to call it quits. He took a deep breath and lay on the bed.

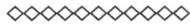

Donald tipped his hat. "Good morning. I have and appointment with Mr. Roberts."

"You are?"

"Donald Page." He stretched his hand forth to shake.

"He'll be right with you. Would you like to sit over there?" The middle-aged woman wiggled her finger.

Donald secured the briefcase in his lap and gave it a pat.

"Hello, Mr. Page?"

Donald stood. "Mr. Roberts? Just call me Donald."

Mr. Roberts scratched his chin. "In that case, drop the *mister*. my first name is also Robert. My mother had some sense of humor."

Donald chuckled as the men walked to the younger man's office.

Looking at the pictures that were spread out, Robert spoke. "This is your friend. The lady you were inquiring about? What's her name?"

Donald let out a long sigh. "Sara. Her name is Sara News." His lips formed a thin line. "Can I see her now?"

"Mr. Page, please sit down." The door shut. "I don't know how to really tell you this." Mr. Roberts sat on the corner edge of the desk. "I don't know if Sara had on a necklace."

"We can perhaps ask her," Donald suggested.

Mr. Roberts shifted. "Donald, late last night Dr. Life made his usual rounds. Sara is one of his patients. Here is his report. It was after visiting hours. Standing outside the unidentified woman's room, I paused to go over her chart. I wanted to record how she was responding after completion of her brain surgery, for she was being monitored."

Donald gasped. "What brain surgery?"

"Here, Donald, take this cup of coffee. It's black and strong."

"Thanks." Donald clung to the warmth.

Mr. Roberts continued the report. "The scan revealed that her brain area was holding water. The doctor tapped in hopes to release the pressure and trying to reduce the swelling." He stood, pressed a button, and paged for Dr. Life.

Dr. Life slowly opened the door after a light tap, and walked into the office. "Hello, Mr. Roberts." He nodded toward Donald. "Sir?"

Donald shakily set his cup down and stood. "Hello. My name is Mr. Donald Page."

"Sir, I hear, and thank you. We have a name for the unidentified woman. What great news.

Donald whispered, "Where's Sara?" He wrung his hands and slumped down. "Dr. Life, can you fill us in on anything else about Sara?"

The doctor looked at Donald with a grim smile, and locked eyes with him. "This Sara has amnesia. It's from an impact she has suffered. As I stepped into her room to examine Sara, she wasn't there she had disappeared. I called the labs to see if she were having late work, but to no avail. She was gone."

"Gone? Gone where?" Donald eyes widened as he gripped the edge of the chair.

Mr. Roberts interjected, "We have filled out a missing person's report, and truthfully, Donald, she could be anywhere. The best knowledge about this is we know her name."

"Would she remember her name?" Donald asked.

"No, Donald. Sometimes these matters heal quickly, and other times, it may take months—years."

"Is it all right if I try the police station?" Donald asked.

"Sure. It's across the street and down two blocks."

"What's your phone number, Donald? Where we can reach you should there be any update on Sara?" Asked the Mr. Roberts.

"I'm at the hotel today, at least." He gathered up Sara's pictures and could hardly mutter, "Thanks."

In the rental car, he bowed his head. "Help!" Tears formed and dropped. He put his hands on the steering wheel. *Poor Sara. Wonder what's happening to her, and where would she be?* Oh my, how was he going to call home and tell them about this mess? Donald pounded the steering wheel. Again he pleaded for Sara. *Watch over her, and bring Sara safely back to us, and thanks.*

He needed a plan of action. On to the police station he drove, and his direction became clear. Donald parked in a visitor's spot. Walking down the hall, he looked for a sign reading "Dispatcher." He took a left and heard a voice drifting, giving directions for a stalled car on the eastside. She glanced up at him.

"May I help you? Are you needing directions?"

Donald stepped in front of the four-inch-round circle designated where one was to speak. "No, thank you, but I do need help. My name is Donald Page, from Ohio. I'm here about a missing woman. Here name would be Sara News."

"Mr. Page, mine is Margie," the woman said. "Mr. Roberts called ahead and said to be expecting you. Can you update me with any information? Just having her name is a good way to begin, and thanks for these updated pictures. We'll get this right out. So far, we have alerted the bus station and train. We also alerted the airport. Donald, we even notified our three cabdrivers. I'm sure it's just a matter of time until she is found. I'm so sorry."

Donald noticed the woman stayed upbeat and sounded sincere. "Mr. Page I'm sure this will turn out with good news. I'm really sorry for you, her family, and friends to be going through with this. It's would not be easy for anyone in this situation. Where are you staying if we should hear anything?"

He heard her type as he spoke. "At the town's hotel for now." He felt drained, and his eye sockets ached. Donald needed to reach the hotel. There were still things he needed to do. He set his mind on a call home before he did anything else. Looking over his shoulder, he said, "Thanks, Margie, for your help and concern." He pulled his coat closer, adjusted his shoulders, and walked out the building.

9

"Hello, Kate? Put me on speakerphone, please. Now gather Karen and Jud if he's there, and, Kate, I'll wait." Donald heard shuffling.

"Donald, this is Jud. We are all here."

"Good. You need to listen, and do not interrupt me. Sit down! Are all of you sitting?"

"Yes. Go ahead."

Shakily, Donald began. "First of all, Kate, I'm fine. Karen, thanks first and foremost for the photos. They really have helped. I met with Mr. Roberts from the hospital, and he offered his full support. I met also with Dr. Life, who took care of Sara, and I have his full report."

"Great," Karen said. "How is she, Dad?"

"Karen, I know it is hard to wait, but shush, dear. Jud, I need Jack's phone number. I'll wait."

"Donald?" Jud asked.

He interrupted and talked over Jud. "We'll talk in a minute, Jud, but now, everyone, Sara has had brain surgery. She had a lot of swelling from water accumulated on her brain."

Kate gasped.

"Quiet please. The surgery was successful." Donald heard clapping in the background. He went on speaking. "Sara has amnesia, and is missing. She up and vanished. I want you to know the police are doing everything possible. They've released a new picture of her on flyers and have notified the bus and train stations and have alerted the airport. They have three cabdrivers here, and they have been informed. All precautions have been set in place. Ladies, I need to talk only with Jud now. Kate, I'll call you later. Keep praying."

The phone clicked.

"Jud, you there?" Donald asked.

"Donald, what the Sam Hill is going on?" Jud wanted to know. "Why don't they know where Sara is? How can someone just disappear?"

"Stop, Jud. Breathe. Tell me what's going on with your work."

What? You want to know about my work?"

"Yes."

"It's complicated," Jud answered. "This was supposed to be a slam dunk case. Spencer, our attorney went before the judge to get the case dismissed, but now the judge wants to reevaluate the land-contract case. Spencer has assured me he went over the case with a fine-tooth comb. He didn't find any loopholes in the contract and thought the case would have been dismissed. He's looking into another strategy. We have to be in court again tomorrow, and Spencer said being this is an election year, the judge may take all week."

"Well, if anyone can work out this case matter, it is Spencer," Donald said. "We need to pray. Now, Jud, what Jack's number?"

"Here it is. Why did you need it?"

"I'm going to ask him if he can join me here at the hotel before going on to Ken's place. He and Louise should know what's happened since their phone lines are still unavailable. Right, Jud? Don't you agree?"

"Donald, Ken's my best friend," Jud said. "I'm very upset I can't even go to him. What's that all about?"

"Jud, you need to stay strong and know who's in charge," Donald said. "Ken is going to need your prayers and lean on you big time."

Exhaling, Jud said, "Donald, your wife is nudging me. She insists she talks with you now."

Donald chuckled. "Put Kate on."

"Honey, are you really all right?" Kate asked. "Are you resting, and how about eating?"

"Kate, Kate, yes. But I do need you to do something for me."

"What, Donald?"

"I need you to wire me some money here at the hotel."

"Give me about an hour. And, Donald, don't try any of those James Bond tricks, you hear?"

He snickered again.

"Bye-bye, Donald."

"I love you, Kate, and thanks."

"Here's Jud."

Donald could hear the car keys rattle, and chuckled, knowing his request would be done.

"Jud, I'm grabbing a bit to eat at the hotel and calling it a night," Donald said. "The first thing in the morning, I will revisit the hospital and see if any updated news or information about Sara has come in. I'll also try to catch Jack. I hope he's back from his trip."

"Me too," Jud said. "I find this all hard to believe."

"I know. Good luck in court tomorrow, Jud. I'll be in touch, but not for a few days. Don't worry, I'm on a mission. You're laughing."

"No, I'm trying not to. I was remembering what Kate warned you not to try. Be careful, Donald, you're in our thoughts. Good night."

Jud was numb, and he felt cold. He paced the floor, knowing he needed to pull himself together for Karen and Kate and Ken, plus there was his work. All this was almost too much for him to digest and handle.

He thought on the information Donald had called about. *Sara had serious surgery, and now she was missing.* He shook his head. *And she doesn't even know who she is.* Jud placed his hands at his temples and rubbed. His head was splitting, and his stomach felt sick.

Jud moved to the kitchen. It was in total quietness. He placed two oversize tablespoons of grounds in the basket and made coffee. He shrugged as he added another spoonful. He wanted it strong, for this was going to be a long night. He paced the floor, waiting and praying for answers, but none floated through the air. He poured a mug of black liquid, brought it to his mouth, blew, and took a sip. He shuddered. It was bitter but satisfying.

Dropping his hands in his lap, he thought, *What is poor Ken going to do, and the boys? Also, there is Sara's mother, Louise.* He remembered Donald said to pray. Jud was brought to the point of dropping on his knees. *All-Knowing One, You are the only answer, and You are ever so needed.*

"Good morning, Mr. Nite. This is Donald Page. I'm so glad I caught you at home."

"Refresh my mind. You are?"

"I am Karen Day's father, Donald. Jud gave me your new number. I wanted to thank your for the concerns you had about the photo of the unidentified woman shown on TV. Well, Jack, it did prove unfortunately to be Sara."

"What? You're kidding."

"No, I'm not kidding. It's the gospel truth. We are just so glad you were watching TV."

Sighing, Donald continued. "Jack, there are new factors concerning Sara—well, several. First, I want you to know that Sara has had brain surgery. Secondly, she is now missing, along with her having amnesia."

"What?" Jack exclaimed.

"There's a lot of details you need to be filled in on, but, Jack, please can you come and join me here in Kentucky? You know Sara so well. I would like for us to do a little search for Sara on our own."

"Donald, I just got back from Brazil. The phone was ringing when I walked through the door. Let me think. There are a few things I need to wrap up here today in the ministry."

"Jack, you're young. You can stretch yourself. Come on and share in this adventure. Most likely we will have to leave from here and fly to Mississippi. It will be a sad day to see poor Ken, Louise, the boys."

Jack let out a long sigh. "What about your son-in-law, Jud? Why isn't he there with you?"

"Glad you asked," Donald replied. "We need to pray for him and his situation. Jud is sick about not being free and able to help. After all, Ken is his best friend. You know that. Our Jud is tied up in court on a land case. It seems the judge has made the case questionable about the signed land contract. Jud's fit to be tied."

"I'm sorry. I should have realized he would be with you. My, what a mess."

"Jack, I could use a friend helping me. Someone walking with God that knows Sara, her family, and friends. She may even respond to you if we find her. Please help." Donald strained his ear against the phone's receiver. Was that a zipper he heard? "Jack, are you there? What are you doing?"

"Gruffly, I'm not unpacking, that's for sure. Maybe I can be of help. I'll call the airport and try to catch a flight out yet tonight. If all goes well, I'll meet you in the hotel lobby by two thirty tomorrow afternoon. Donald, have the coffee ready—black. See you there. Bye, Mr. Page."

"Bye, Mr. Nite, and thank you."

Donald inhaled his sandwich and dragged his body to his room. He showered and was still droopy. He saw his bedsheet turned down. He showered and picked up his Bible. Reading the twenty-third Psalms was comforting and helpful. He slid under the cover and closed his eyes. *Thank you, Lord, and good night.*

There was a knock on Donald's door. He jerked and hollered, "Just a minute." He checked his back pocket, pulling out his wallet, and opened the door.

"Mr. Page?" It was the bellhop.

"Yes."

"The switchboard has a call from a Jud. Your son-in-law is on the line. Do you wish to take the call?"

Donald nodded and gave the bellhop fifty cents.

"Thanks, Mr. Page."

Donald took off his shoes and wiggled his toes. "Hello, Jud. Wait just a minute, and let me sit down. Now fill me in on what's happening there."

"Donald, I stepped out of the court room to make a brief call," Jud said. "Did you reach Jack? Is he going to come and help?"

"Jud, the answer to both questions is yes. He's due here today in the afternoon, around two thirty."

"Great news. Call me when you can, Donald. They are motioning me back into the court room."

"I will. Keep praying. Good-bye."

Jud was gone.

Donald changed clothes and was having his devotions when there was a sharp knock on the door. A bellman appeared, and Donald was happy for the interruption. He took the tray, and he gave the bellman a tip. He smelled the black coffee and thought, *Looks can be so deceiving.* The open-face split-egg sandwich was good but chewy. The potatoes were hard, but the coffee was excellent.

The morning turned into afternoon, and Donald was waiting in the lobby of the hotel for Jack. He didn't disappoint him, for at 2:30 p.m. sharp, in walked Jack.

"Hello, Jack," Donald greeted. "So glad you could make it. I have your things taken to my room and ordered another bed."

They shook hands, settled with arrangements, and headed to the hospital. It was still a mystery as to where Sara went. No news has been forward to the hospital, and none was updated at the police station.

Donald said, "Jack, I'll call Jud and see if they have heard anything from Ken. If not, we ought not to wait any longer. We should head for Mississippi. Someone needs to face Ken and Louise and let them know about Sara."

"Donald, do you want me to check and see if we can get a flight out to Mississippi today?" Jack asked.

"Sure, Jack. Please do so just as soon as I make this call."

The phone rang.

"Hello, this is Jud."

"Jud, this is Donald. I'm fine, and Jack is here with me. There hasn't been any change with any information. Have you heard anything?"

"Not a word, Donald. Nothing. The lines are still down in Mississippi."

"I was afraid of that. Well, Jack and I are checking in about a flight there today after this call. Jud, we think you better call Ken's father and mother." Donald let out a sigh. "Maybe this is God's plan to bring Ken closer to his family."

"Sir, it may well be," Jud agreed. "I'll take care of calling his dad."

"How's your court case going?" Donald heard a smacking sound and thought, *Jud hit the counter.*

"The judge is supposed to make his decision tomorrow," Jud answered. I pray we win. This whole mess could have been settled out of court. Election year, really."

"Just pray. He's the only answer, Jud. You know Spencer is the best in his line of work. Take care. I'll talk with you when we can get this settled at Ken's. Say hi to the family and Kate. Bye, Jud. I love you."

"Love you too, Donald."

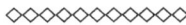

"Hello, this is Jon."

"Sir, this is Judwin Day."

"Jud, what on earth? This is sure a pleasant surprise to hear from you." The chair squeaked as Jon sat down. "What's going on, Jud?"

"Jon, I'm calling about some unpleasant news. I'm sorry to be the one sharing this. It's about Sara."

Jon interjected, "What about Sara?"

"She was here in Ohio for a visit, and also to pursue her new business. She departed on time by flight, and there was a twister of wind and rain. Her mother, Louise, decided to move to Mississippi, so she left Ohio with Ken and the boys." Jud let out a sigh. "I really don't mean to prattle."

"What are you talking about, boy?" Jon asked.

"Ken made a surprise visit to our place to help celebrate Sara's success in her business," Jud asked. "He drove a rental from Mississippi, but Sara flew. Sara's plane was caught in a storm and went down."

Jon gasped. "What? Oh my. How's Ken?"

"Jon, Sara is alive, but has amnesia. She also had water on her brain. An emergency surgery was required."

"Where is she? What hospital? We'll go. Poor Ken, Louise, and the boys."

"Jon, there's more. Sara is now missing from the hospital, and since the lines are down in Mississippi, Ken and her mother know nothing." Jud breathed. "Donald and Jack are headed to Mississippi to inform your son and Louise now, as we speak."

"My word."

"Jon, I have been dealing with a bank court case, and I'm not happy that it has not allowed me to be there for my friend. I'm so sorry, Jon."

"Jud, I'll let his mother know as soon as she returns from the grocery store," Jon promised. "We'll make our arrangements today and drive to Mississippi. We need to be there for him, the boys, and poor Louise. First, her husband, and now this. It's so terrible."

Jud let out a long sigh. "Ken is going to need all the support he can get."

"I know he will. I'll let Ken know about the court case and how unavoidable it has turned out for you not to be able to come. Now, Jud, you win this case, boy, and call us as soon as Ken's lines are up. And thank you for calling us. See you, Jud. Bye."

11

"Well, good morning, my new shy friend." Claudia patted the kitchen barstool. "Hop up here, and eat your breakfast."

Sara stretched her arms overhead, yawning. "How long did I sleep, Claudia?"

Claudia smiled, while placing a napkin under the fork. "Missy, you were out the minute your head hit the big fluffy feather pillow. It's now been twenty-four hours. You've slept around the clock."

"My goodness." She paused. "Thanks for the eggs and toast. They hit the spot." She walked to the coffeepot and went to pour a cup. She held the cup in midair. "Claudia, do you have any tea?"

Claudia bit her lip, reached into the cupboard, and handed her a tea bag. "I'll heat the water for you." She put a pan of water on the wood burning stove and waited for it to boil.

"You want any sugar or cream to go with your tea?" Claudia continued. "Dr. Life will be glad things worked out for me to bring you here to the farm. I hadn't been sure they would give me the time off when I first asked after last week, but it was nice to see the request answered and placed in my in box at the nurses' station."

The cup was set down, and Sara looked around. "Thank you for helping me. It was really dark last night when we arrived, and I couldn't make out your place. You seemed to have driven for a long time off the main highway before we stopped. Was that your driveway?"

Claudia smacked her hand on her leg. "Yep, it's a far piece off the road, all right, but I like privacy, and it is posted 'Keep off.'" She took a cloth and began wiping the counter. "My hired hand took a few days off, so I'll be doing the chores. Maybe you'll get to see the new foal that's due when it is born. Later today, I'll show you around. You need to lie back down for a while now." She turned. "I hope you rest and enjoy your stay." She flipped her hands forward, encouraging her guest to take the step and lie down.

"Claudia, I really am not sleepy."

"Try reading. Just rest. You know you have been through quite a trauma."

"Can you stay and visit with me for a while?"

They walked to her room, and Claudia sat in the oversize chair. "It was really late, missy, when we left last night. Gathering your meds and paperwork was not fun. I also regret the way I had to leave my work form and request for the one-month leave from work with the night guard. He sometimes can be a little forgetful."

Lazily, her patient yawned. "Did you give him my permission slip for me to leave the hospital?"

"Yes, I did, along with sharing with him that I was bringing you with me to the farm."

She nodded.

Hitting her knee, Claudia belted out, "Hey, are you all right with me calling you Jane?"

She frowned. "I don't think Jane fits me. It doesn't sound right, but what do I know. I guess I don't mind. Can I call you Clo?"

"How on earth did you come up with a name like that?"

"Oh, it sounds sweet, and that's what you are." She yawned again, and her eyes fluttered.

Claudia ruffled her guest's hair. "What a fine pair we make." She pushed herself up, shook her head, and slowly closed the door.

Claudia left a note by the coffee Drip-O-lator, stating she would be at the barn. It was time for chores.

Claudia turned the radio on low. She remembered reading somewhere animals like music. She picked up the fifty-pound bag of oats, slinging it over her shoulder. There was the feeding, watering, and stalls to be cleaned. Then it would be time to walk then brush the horses down. Work never got done on the farm.

She kept a sharp eye on her mare, for she was snarling and being fidgety. She would paw the ground and whinny. Claudia talked with her and rubbed her neck, trying to calm her down.

She shooed the chickens out from the barn and threw their cracklings to them. They clucked and spread their wings, until the Big Red appeared. He strutted his stuff, crowed, and all the hens bowed their heads. Claudia shoved her hand in her bib pockets, tossed her head back, and laughed.

Claudia turned and saw Jane approach. What a sight. She had on a twirl skirt, a buttoned-up blouse and three-inch heels.

Claudia cleared her throat. "Hi, baby girl. Did you have a nice rest?" She walked and joined Jane in the yard. "Let's try different shoes."

Jane nodded and looped an arm into Claudia's, flashing her a wide smile.

"Now isn't that better?"

"They're flats, Claudia."

"I know that. You don't have any kind of tie shoe, and you need ties for outside."

Jane shrugged. "Okay, I'll wear these for now."

"Hungry?" Claudia asked.

She tilted her head to the side. "Surprisingly, I am a little."

They went to the kitchen. Claudia poured beans in the pan and laid hot dogs on the counter. "Jane, I made some ice tea. You want brown sugar, or do I leave it unsweetened?"

"I don't know how I like it," Jane answered. "Let's try with one lump of sugar."

"Jane, use your spoon," Claudia instructed. "There, see? Scoop the granule of sugar. Now stir."

"This seems strange, but the tea tastes good."

Clearing the table, Claudia said, "I'll take a look at the surgical area and change your head dressing. We'll plan to see Dr. Life in two weeks. I'm sure he'll run a few more tests and see how you are doing. Looks clean."

"My head is sore, but I don't have a headache now."

"That's good, Jane. How was your walk to the barn?"

She laughingly stated, "I was wobbling because of the heeled shoes."

"Jane, want to try again? Do you feel strong enough?"

"Clo, maybe if I hold on to you."

Slowly they reached the barn.

"Clo, this looks like a petting zoo."

How did she know that?

"Hogs, sheep, goats, chickens, and horses. I feel at home. Oh, look at the little one."

"Jane, foals don't usually take right up with people when they are first born. You're a natural with animals. Do you think you own any horses?"

"I don't know. Nothing comes to mind." Jane puckered up, and punched her hand.

"Well, let's head for the house," Claudia said. "I want you to take it easy for the next few days. Jane, you need lots of rest. As you feel stronger and your walk becomes steadier, you can help me with a few chores if you want to. Maybe in a week or two we can try riding."

"Clo, how much land do you own?" Jane asked.

"Child, as far as your eye can see, and then further." Claudia scratched her head. "I own about a hundred and ninety-seven acres. One of the farmers came and sowed the front and side yards with bluegrass when I first moved here. The back here, well, it's whatever comes up, and it's mostly clover and weeds."

Claudia stretched her hands outward. "I own twenty-three racehorses and have won many races. I have a showcase full of prizes. I have bred, bought, and raised the top of the lines. My stallions are from the best stock of their breed."

Jane walked over to the showcase. "Are these your trophies and ribbons?"

Claudia glanced and saw sparkles in Jane's eyes. She nodded. "Let's sit on the porch for a little while." Claudia carried out baloney sandwiches to eat and cool creamed milk for them to drink. "Here are your meds. Jane, in an hour, you'll need to lay back down for a while."

They swung in silence. Claudia kept thinking of all the chores she needed to be doing. She saw Jane's eyed batting. "Come on, little one, so you can rest." Claudia placed the ringer down on the phone so if anyone called it would go straight to the answering machine. She didn't want anything to disturb her patient.

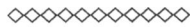

A week and a half passed. Jane was feeling better, and her bandages were almost ready to come off for good.

"Clo, I'll just watch you ride, but thanks for asking," she said. "I would rather watch."

Swatting her hat, Claudia thought, *This woman must be a city slicker. Her hands are soft and her skin is smooth.*

Jane followed Claudia around like a leech. She got to know each horse by name. She seemed to enjoy feeding them. She would brush and walk the horses when it was necessary, but she had a faraway look in her eyes.

Claudia shook her head. Poor Jane. She would ask the same questions, not remembering she has just asked the same one. But Claudia would smile and repeat the answers over again.

Claudia placed her tanned hand to her forehead. It was great having company. Claudia had not felt she was lonely before for a long, long time—not until now.

Another week passed, and Jane was now able to saddle and get upon a horse. She would only let the horse walk and sometimes trot.

Claudia and Jane rode out near the end of her southern area one evening to have a picnic. Sitting there, Jane spread her hands out. "This is beautiful. Seeing the sunset and hearing the water roar in the creek. It is simply breathtaking."

"You know I never get tired of this myself."

"Claudia, do you have a boyfriend?"

Claudia hit her hat on her lap. "Shucks, no. What made you think of that question?"

"Claudia, this is a huge place, even with a ranch hand," Jane said. "With your work and all, I thought you would have someone to share this with."

Claudia let out a long breath. She felt at ease with her new patient. Even knowing she should stay professional, she felt a tug deep in her heart for Jane. "Well, a long time ago, there was someone special. We met each other baling hay. After a year, I would meet up with him monthly and enjoy a dip of ice cream. But that all changed. He took a job up north, said he was going to send for me, but I know it was hard for him find stable work. It wasn't as easy as he had thought.

"After he left in two weeks, I received my first letter from him. Oh, at first he wrote every week, and then it dwindled to every once in a while and finally not at all. All my letters came back unopened." She looked at Jane. "Shameful, I know, but after another month passed, I made the trip to the address that was on his last letter."

Claudia rocked back and forth and took Jane's hand. "He didn't live there." A tear threatened to slide down. Claudia bit her lip. "He had never lived there. The address was to a country store. The store owner was a rude dried-up old man. He said a man named Charles collected some letters there, and one day, a long-legged woman stopped in. The woman came across as brazen and asked Charles to leave with her. The store owner saw him nod and smile. Charles picked up his tattered suitcase, opened the car door, sat his case on the backseat, and got into her car. The store owner said they were laughing and holding hands. He shook his head. Charles never wrote, called, or returned to the town.

"I stood there feeling numb and stupid. When I returned home, I enrolled into nursing at my parents' request. It was right before graduation my parents died from fever. I couldn't stand it, so I sold their place and bought this ranch. Later, I returned to school and finished. I was hired on at the hospital with top honors.

"Living here is meaningful, but I never gave it a thought to feel anything else for anyone else, I guess until I met you. You were like a wounded animal needing help and care. I thought at first it was because of my training as a nurse. I prayed for your recovery. What I have noticed is how nice it is to have conversations and they are not all about my work."

Gathering their things, Jane had tears threatening to fall. "I'm sorry, Clo, for your pain, but God may have someone yet for you. It just hasn't been the right time. You need to open your heart up again."

Riding the horses back, Claudia looked at Jane and pondered. *Is there a man somewhere for me, or is it too late? Don't think like that, Claudia. See where the first time it got you.*

"Pray, Clo, and I will too," Jane said.

The chores were painfully done. Jane had her meds and was fast asleep. Claudia walked out onto the porch and put her hand on the rail. *Hey, up there, this Jane down here needs You, and so do I. Is there someone for me, or am I being stupid again? We'll talk later, I know You are busy. Oh, it's Claudia.*

She kicked off her boots and locked up for the night. She headed to the kitchen to check the answering machine to see if anyone had called.

Things progressed with Jane. It had been slow, but she was beginning to have bits and pieces of recall. She remembered a tall man with long hair and how he made her feel safe. His skin was smooth, and his hands were large.

Jane had told Claudia about him on one of her rides. Jane found she loved to ride and was good doing it.

"Want to take a ride to the west side of the land, Jane?" Claudia asked.

"Sure. Let me get saddled up."

Claudia held the horse as Jane hopped on. "You make me feel safe too, Claudia. Thank you." She swept her hat around. "Let's ride like the wind."

The horses galloped, and the land was breathtaking. Its ground of blue-green seemed to stretch out into the blue in the sky.

"Clo, stop," Jane said suddenly.

Claudia slowed down to a trot. "What?"

"Someone has a round-form necklace and was touching it when I left to board a plane. Where was I going or coming from?" She held her head. "It's like mine." She felt at her throat. "Do you have my necklace, Claudia?" Her mind wondered. *I don't like planes.*

Tears formed in Claudia's eyes. "Yes, I have the necklace. This is good, things popping up in the head. I'm proud of you. Let's turn now and go back to the barn. Slowly this time."

They went back to the barn.

"Here's your meds, and I'll take another look at your head," Claudia said. She inspected Jane's head. "Well, the area is mostly healed, and your hair has begun growing back."

Jane pounded her fists. "When am I going to remember my life?"

"You're tired. Too much riding?"

"No, just wondering about my necklace."

Claudia excused herself and came back in the room with the necklace. "Here, Jane. You had this on when I was seated next to you on the plane."

"Plane? What was I doing on a plane?" Jane began to shake fearfully.

Claudia handed her a cup of steaming tea as she set hers down.

"I want to go to bed now, Clo!" Jane said.

"Need any help?" Claudia asked.

"Not tonight, but thank you." Jane walked the steps, fingering the necklace as she did so.

"Call me if you need me, baby girl."

Claudia slipped outside on the porch, feeling a deep disturbance. She marched around the wraparound porch. As far as her eyes could see was her land. She seized a seat in the swing. It used to be so satisfying knowing what she owned. She listened as the birds settled in for the night. Shaking her head, she thought how it was only a few days ago that hearing the birds chirp or looking at the bluest grass or seeing her registered horses fulfilled her. Hitting her leg, she said to the air, "Stop it, you old slob. You'll be blubbering like an old cow who lost its calf."

She wiped her eyes with the back of her sleeve. Why was this strange frustration trying to creep in? *Maybe residing to be an old maid was wrong. A little late for that, Claudia Bronk,* she thought. A few more tears were shed before she blew her nose. She kicked the ground and gave herself a lecture.

Once more, Claudia looked at the horizon. The sun skirted with a wink behind the earth in a dip, as if it were saying good night.

11

Karen and Kate were busy making purses. They finished the last zipper on the thirty-sixth purse. They admired the varieties.

Karen heard the mailman. She checked, and sure enough, he had brought her another booked show. She marched straight into the office and showed her mother.

On the computer, Karen clicked onto the file and updated the amount received from the show. One column showed customers' purchase, and another column showed how many bookings also if they were live shows or bookings requests.

Kate watched over Karen's shoulder. "Who could have imagined how successful Sara's business adventure would be?"

"Well, I'm glad the remodeling here to convert part of the parlor over for a storefront is done. The purses have really sold. What a success, and poor Sara." Karen sighed. "Mom, I wonder where she is and if anyone is helping her. It's more than I can stand."

Tears formed, and Kate passed Karen a stack of hankies as she blew her nose. "Karen, you need to pull yourself together and run this business for Sara. Don't you have another hostess to call for confirmation of a show, and aren't there others to reach that you heard from today? Now blow." Kate passed Karen the phone.

"Mom, can you watch the twins for me tonight again? Jud is so tied up with this case. I left his meal in the warmer knowing it couldn't be too good, but he must be eating, for the plate was empty and he was gone when I got up."

"Karen, sure I will watch the twins with delight. I think I will take them to the park. I know what you mean about Jud being gone. I hope this ruling goes in the bank's favor, or Jud will be a mess." Kate walked to the sink. "Karen, there is a note in here for you. It's from Jud."

Karen left the office and rushed to the kitchen. Her mother handed her a cup of brewed tea with a lump of sugar and the note. She unfolded it.

Dear sweet Karen,

I miss you, and I love you. Thanks for being so wonderful and understanding about the time I am spending on this case.

I know things are hard on you with your best friend missing and the purse shows, and taking care of Luke and Luci, but you are strong, and I know you are a prayer warrior. Remember, He cares. Things will work out.

Maybe we can get away and go to Sara's and Ken's place when this is over. We'll talk later. Thank you, darling.

Love,
Jud

"Karen, I'm glad both of you worked out your differences," Kate said. "You seem so close now. No secrets?"

"No, Mom." Karen turned pink. "Only open communication."

Kate patted her hand. "You better hurry. The show can't begin without you. Want me to help pack the green bomber?"

Karen heard the wonderful voices blending in.

"I will help, Mommy."

Karen turned toward the stairway. "Thanks, Luke and Luci. Work with Grandma. Okay? She is taking you both to the park. I'll miss you."

"Can we wait up for you, Mommy?" Luci asked.

"Come on, you two," Kate said. "Let's get your mom's show equipment loaded. Let's see—purses, forms, pens, and pins. All set. Then we'll see about tonight, Luci."

It was an unbelievably dark and dreary day. Already, big drops of rain were falling. Karen shuddered as she sat behind the computer. She touched her penny swear necklace before she updated the show's monies and compared the loss and gain on the work chart. She needed to note what went out on supplies and materials. She stared at the figures. Wow. She saw a profit of two hundred dollars. She must write this down and save the information for Sara.

Karen glanced out the window and saw the sun trying to peek though the gray clouds that covered the sky. The rain was still falling, but a promise of a rainbow was trying to appear. Karen bowed her head and gave thanks.

She stared at the computer again and switched programs for her to view the bed-and-breakfast business. She sighed. It was just holding its own. She tapped her fingers on the desk. If only she could get September and October completely booked, she would be on the plus.

She thought, *There are always customers dropping in during November and December.* Karen stared at the charts. The first half of next year was extremely booked. She would soon need to decide if she were going to do additional advertising for the bed-and-breakfast.

Pushing up from the desk, Karen ventured to the kitchen. The twins would soon be up, and Jud was gone again. She read the note left on the refrigerator.

> Good morning, Karen. I've gone over to Louise's house. I will be there most of the day. Louise had wanted me to get a list of furniture she had left behind and call an auction house to dispose of it.
>
> Jud mentioned last night while you were at the show that he had received two possible buyers' contracts for

Louise's house. He is in negotiations with Mr. Drum and should have some information soon to give Ken.

Karen, he will be home late again tonight also, and so will I. It's just you and the kids. Your father is joining me to help with the inventory.

See you later, and have fun.

Love,
Mother

Karen heard Luke and Luci talking as they rushed down the stairs. "Good morning, you two."

"Where's Grandma?" said Luke.

Rattling the dishes and reaching for the casserole dish, Karen said, "Grandma is over at Louise's house, working. It's just you and me today."

"You have any shows to do?" said Luci.

"No, but I have a surprise."

Together, they spoke. "What, Mommy?"

"Well, first, Luke, will you get the glass dish for me under that shelf? Luci, if you hand me the vegetables, we can get them washed and cut. We'll make the chicken casserole dish and turn the oven on low. Then I will let you know what we are going to do."

The twins were busy with the rattling of pans and the opening and shutting the refrigerator door. Karen slid her hands down her apron and smiled at how helpful her twins had gotten.

"Mommy, we're done," Luci said. "What are we doing today?"

"Right, Mommy," Luke chimed in. "Are we going somewhere?" His eyes sparkled, Karen giving a pleading look.

Karen untied her apron. "I have three tickets for the variety dog show. They will be dressed in fancy suits and strutted with their owners around the big ring. Maybe do some tricks. Anyone want to go?"

The twins nodded and had a huge smile come on their faces, as did Karen. "Well, let's get ready and meet back here in the kitchen in twenty minutes. We only have two hours from now to get there."

Approaching the stairway, Ken took the steps two at a time. His hair flowed as it was not quite dry. "Mom, Dad, what are you doing here, coming out in this terrible weather? Is everything all right?"

Jon hesitated, shifted, and poked Sylvia.

Sylvia held out her arms and hugged her son. "Yes, the rain is coming down and the roads are somewhat washed out, but you know your father, he'll plow through anything if we want to go."

Ken cocked his head. "Dad, is this an essential visit?"

Jon half smiled and patted his son's shoulder. "Louise informed us of her stay with you, and about the mare. Did you get her settled?"

Louise called everyone into the kitchen. She placed a snack tray on the table and poured coffee. Sylvia greeted Louise in the kitchen, and Ken, with Jon, followed.

The lights had come on, but they were still flickering. No words were spoken. Only the sips of coffee could be heard.

Louise took Sylvia's hand. "Come, I'll show you the room where you and Jon will be staying."

Sylvia's eyes widened and were in question, but she followed the lead. Their voices carried as they walked the long hall.

"Here is a candle and the snuffer," Louise said. "The matches are in your dresser drawer in the left top area."

Sylvia clutched the hangers given to her by Louise and shook them.

"I'm glad you're here, Sylvia," Louise said. "This house seems eerie without Sara. I just don't know what's holding her up. I've a strange feeling mulling in my heart."

Sylvia all but threw the hangers down and grabbed Louise. She kept silent, but the hug lasted a long time.

Louise briskly walked toward the kitchen and overheard Ken converse with his father. Ken was explaining about the new room additions he planned on building for Sara's business. Ken unfolded himself and padded on the floor in his bare feet.

Softly, Louise interjected. "Ken, Jon, it's late, and tomorrow is another day. Why don't we all retire? Five a.m. comes early." She looked at Ken then Jon. She tapped her foot, instructing Jon to take the first left after the living room and turn at the first bedroom. "Sylvia is in waiting."

Ken hunched his shoulders and peeked out the window before trying the phone. He raked his hair back into a ponytail and shook his head. There wouldn't be any sun in the morning, for the rain was still coming down in sheets. He tapped the phone. The line was still dead, and the lights flickered again as he resorted to the flashlight.

He didn't know when Louise had made coffee or how, but taking a mug of hot joe on the run was warm and agreeable. He slipped into his slickers and boots as he tried shielding his face against the wind. Sam called out to him in the morning's dreariness while flagging the iron lantern.

Sam and Ken were just finishing mucking the stalls. Ken saw the oat's feedbag near the wall. The horses were stomping and making whiny sounds, letting him know they were waiting.

Jon placed a hand on the barn door. "Hey, Ken. You sure have improved your spread."

Ken nodded as he handed a pail of oats to his dad to help feed. "Dad, this is Sam. He's my right-hand man. Sam, this is my father, Jon."

"Pleased to meet you, sir," Jon said.

"Likewise." Sam smiled and began whistling some offbeat tune while he brushed and groomed one mare at a time.

Ken walked over to his new mare. "I'm disappointed in you, Missy. I think breeding is in store for you. It might even settle you down and hopefully keep you at home."

Sam glanced up. "Your neighbor got a new stud yesterday. The winds must have carried his smell."

Jon lifted one foot then the other. "Ken, do you already have the lumber for the new addition? Since I'm here, I can be of help if you want." He raised a hand. "You know my trade. Besides, your mother and I needed to see you."

Ken raised his eyebrows to one. He looked into his dad's eyes. Something was there, but what? "Dad, all the material is here. It's in the side shed over there." He pointed. "I think we'll have to wait until the rain stops to be able to work, though."

Jon asked, "May I see the plans? There are some things I can do now."

Ken hunched his shoulders and looked down at his dad. "Be my guest."

By afternoon, the rain had moved on. Ken and Jon were working side by side. The only noise heard was from a saw or a hammer.

Louise and Sylvia looked at the men's work while Timmy and Matthew were resting.

Sylvia smiled as Ken glanced her way, winking. "It's nice to see my men working together, Ken. You are a natural just like your father when it comes to carpentry work." She clapped. "It's a real art."

"Sara is going to be so surprised." Louise bit her lip.

Sylvia said, "Come on, Louise, let's get to the house. There's dinner to make, and the men are heavy eaters."

Jon kept working, never breaking a sweat. "I need the hammer, Dad."

"You need a four-inch screw then a nail, Ken." Jon put his hands in his pockets. "How's the bank business doing?"

Ken stretched. "It's good. When the rain stops, there's supposed to be a CEO meeting." He pulled off his tool belt. "Dad, we've got a lot done today. Thanks."

Jon nodded. "Ken, can we go in town tonight and eat? Your mother and I need to talk with you. Bring the boys along if you want. Might be nice."

"Formal or casual, Dad?"

"Casual. Is there a place close by?"

"Dad, I don't want to alarm Mom or Louise, but I'm concerned about Sara," Ken said. "I know the planes play havoc in the rainy season sometimes." He adjusted his hat. "It's going on twenty-eight hours, and still no word from her."

"Ken, the phones line are up and working now," Louise hollered out. "The man down the way just called about his stallion and your mare. I told him you'd call him back."

Ken looked over his shoulder. "Sam."

"I'm on it, boss," Sam said.

Walking to the house, Jon began unbuttoning his jacket. "Ken, we came here on a mission, and of course, we wanted to see you and the boys. Your mother and I have serious news to give you from Donald and your old study teacher, Mr. Nite."

"What's it about?"

The phone rang again. Ken answered. "Hello? J. J.?"

The phone clicked on speaker. "Hello, I'm back from New York, and I'm here at the bank. I opened for business. Hey, how did it feel to be a teller again?"

A chuckle slid out. "Being a teller came back like riding a bike."

"Ken, there's a letter here for you," J. J. said. "It's from Jud."

"I need you to open it and read it to me," Ken said.

"It says you need to pull every file pertaining to contracts on land purchases. 'I'll see you tomorrow first thing, and tell J. J. to be there at 7:00 a.m.'" He gasped. "Why so early?"

"To get caught up, J. J.," Ken said. "You need to pull the files—all of them, as Jud instructed. Then you need to check with Spencer and see if he is still coming next month, or is he due here tomorrow? We need to plan and be organized!"

J. J. sighed. "Ken, I'll take care of business."

"Tomorrow then. Glad you're back. Bye, J. J." Ken turned to Louise. "Sorry about supper tonight. Can you store the meal you're fixing for tomorrow?"

"Sure, but why?" Louise asked.

"Dad and Mom are taking the boys and me out to eat. Want to come along, Louise?"

"Thanks, but no. I'll stay here in case Sara calls."

There wasn't time to make any calls, for the day had turned into evening. Ken drove to the local diner. The service went smoothly. The huge hamburger sandwiches tasted like a fine chef's steak. The boys finished and spotted some friends and wanted to go talk with them. Ken nodded, and the boys went to the other people's table. They acknowledged him with a smile.

Jon gazed at Sylvia, and she nudged him. Jon cleared his throat. "Son, Jud has tried to reach you by phone and computer, but because of Mississippi's weather havoc, it was impossible." Jon scrunched his brow and sighed. "Jud wanted to come here himself but was tied up with a court case."

Jon moved his chair. "Jud called your mother and me, for he obtained some information about Sara." He placed a hand on Ken's forearm. "I know you are totally confused, and I'm not saying this very well or clear. When we get home, you'll understand why Sara has not made it home."

Their eyes locked.

"Donald and Jack have news on Sara, and they are on their way to your house as we speak," Jon said.

Ken straightened in his chair, never losing eye contact with his dad. He asked through gritted teeth, "What? Do you still think I'm that irresponsible person and can't handle anything so you butted in and came, thinking you would take care of me?" Unfolding his arms and forming his hands into fists, he sternly said, "Tell me what about Sara's delay."

Jon touched his son's arm and, thin lipped, answered, "First, I—*we* never thought you couldn't handle Sara's being missing. I wanted to be here for you and give moral support."

Ken clutched at his throat. "Has something happened to her?"

"Ken, Donald and Jack have followed up with the news about Sara," Donald said. "They will have answers to all of your—*our* questions. Son, your mother and I only want to help."

Sylvia stood, softly touching Ken's shoulder. He looked into her eyes and saw tears forming.

Ken tried to stand. He needed to get the boys and go home, but his legs wouldn't move. He tried again for leg support, but the room went spinning. "Dad, help me. I need some air." His breathing became raspy.

Jon retrieved his wallet and laid money on the table. There was enough for the bill, besides a large tip. Jon placed his arm around his son's waist, but Ken still did not move. He tried talking with him, but Ken was slowly slumping.

Jon took a deep breath, closed his eyes, and slapped Ken's cheek. He silently beckoned Sylvia to get the boys. Jon motioned to the car, clutching Ken's arm and leading him outside. Jon leaned Ken against the car to slide him into the passenger's seat. He lifted Ken's legs and shut the door.

The boys and Sylvia sat in the backseat behind the driver's side, and she began singing. Ken saw his dad behind the wheel making adjustments to the mirrors and the seat. The engine started, and his dad pulled out from the gravel driveway. He was headed home to the ranch.

12

Louise thumped the farmer's sink and sighed. *Wonder where my Sara could be?* She hung her apron on a hook and laid the towel over the line. She listened. It was quiet. Only the crickets were chirping.

She padded down the hall and turned on the bathwater. It was nice to have some alone time. She added the oils and bubble salts and placed her toe in the water. *Just right.* She slid beneath the bubbles.

She loved a claw-foot tub. She felt so relaxed and refreshed. As she dried off, she put a plan of action in thought. She would put on a fresh pot of coffee and would make herself a pot of tea. Maybe even warm a piece of cherry pie and add a dip of vanilla ice cream on it. Her mouth was watering.

Louise slid her granny gown over head and shimmied into it. She covered with a terry cloth robe and shoved her feet into cozy slippers. She ventured into the kitchen and stretched to turn the radio on low. She whirled to the tune sang by Frank Sinatra. *What a crooner.*

The teapot whistled, and the coffeepot wisped. Louise cut and placed the warm cherry sweet on the table and poured herself a cup of freshly brewed tea.

She blew and took a sip. It made her think of Karen and the many teas she brewed. Louise forked her sweet and closed her eyes. She relished in the moment her lips would meet their pleasure.

Suddenly, a loud banging knock came from the front door. She gasped. "Hold your horses. I'm coming." She placed her uneaten bite of pie on the plate and yelled, "I'm coming!"

It was probably Sara. She must have forgotten her key. Louise smiled and opened the wide heavy oak door. "Hello." Her jaw dropped. "What are you two doing here?"

"Well, hello. We're glad to see you too, Louise."

There were two men on the porch.

Louise put her hand to her face. "I'm sorry. Where's my manners? Come in. Would you like a cup of tea or coffee? May I take your coats?"

Donald answered, "Coffee would be nice."

They slid out from their coats and handed them to Louise.

"Follow this way, gentlemen," Louise said.

"Ma'am, call me Jack, and I would surely enjoy a cup of hot tea."

"Black is fine for me." Donald raised his cup.

"Donald, Jack, are you here on bank business or on updates from Karen's shows?" Louise asked.

"No. It's personal. We are here to see you and Ken. We have some facts concerning Sara." Answered Jack.

"Ken's out with Jon and Sylvia and the boys," Louise said. "What news? Where is she?"

The back door closed with a bang. It was Ken.

"Hello, Ken, take a seat. Mrs. News, bring Ken a cup of coffee too. Please."

Donald began. "There isn't any easy way for us to tell you, Ken, Louise, and boys, but…"

"Tell me what?" Ken took a sip of coffee.

"Timmy, Matthew, come with Grandma," Louise said. "Let's get ready for bed. I'll read to you."

Only the sound of scampering feet was heard. Silence filled the air.

Donald took a sip of his drink. "The flight your wife was on had trouble. It crashed. Everyone on the plane survived with only scrapes and bruises."

Ken let out a sigh and went paler.

"Jud wanted to be here in person, but matters had tied him up in court. He sends his regards for not being here for you." Donald pointed to Jack and himself. "We're the next best ones next to your mother and father."

"Did the people from the plane need to go to the hospital?" Ken asked. "Where is Sara?"

Donald leaned forward. "Yes, all the people went in groups to the hospital to be checked out. All that is except Sara, we think."

Jack spoke and gave the name of the hospital, but he didn't say whether Sara was with the group or not. "Ken, we didn't know until yesterday about your wife."

"What?" Ken asked.

"Her paperwork from the plane was lost," Jack replied. "The hospital had a picture of a woman flashed on TV. I saw it, thinking it looked a lot like Sara, and called Jud. That's how I learned your phone lines were down."

Quietly Louise entered the room and pour her a cup of coffee and listened to the men talk.

Ken raked a hand through his hair. "Why didn't Sara just tell them who she is?"

"Sara has amnesia from the landing," Jack said. "She went in a separate ambulance to the hospital without any paperwork."

Donald clutched at Ken's hands. "Let us try to bring you up to date. Jack and I went to the hospital and were able to show the hospital a recent photo of Sara, and they identified her."

"Well, I need to get the first flight out of here," Ken said. "Sara must be frightened to death. She has no one." Tears tumbled down his face.

Louise sat weeping and Sylvia tried to comfort her.

Donald cleared his throat again. "Sit down, Ken. Listen to me. You will not be going to the hospital to see Sara."

"Just why not, sir?"

"She's not there now."

"Where is Sara? I'll go to her."

Donald stood. "Just sit there and listen to me. Sara is now missing from the hospital. As we speak, they are checking all the records and asking questions of every staff member. Their search for Sara will not stop until each person has been questioned and she is found."

Donald stood up and paced. "Jack and I have built a relationship with Dr. Roberts and have been working with him. We are to fly back there tomorrow and meet up with him early. Now, Ken, we will call you with any updates or information we collect."

Jack touched Ken's shoulder and softly spoke. "We came here personally because your phone lines were down, and Jud wanted and asked your parents to be here with you and Louise when you found out about Sara. I'm sorry, Ken and Louise, for our coming and bringing this dreadful news to you."

Ken grabbed a surprised Louise and buried his face into her shoulder, crying and shaking like a child. "What am I to do?"

Louise rocked him back and forth, stroking his hair and mouthing soothing words. Her eyes were closed, and they knew she was talking to the Most Powerful One.

The ride into the doctor's office was quiet.

Claudia spoke up. "I think your stitches will come out today. Come on, now, don't be afraid. I'm here with you."

"I'm scared," Jade confessed.

"Now you have to be a brave person. You've ridden a horse, and didn't know if you had ever ridden before. And you're gaining some memory. It will come."

Claudia held on to Jane's elbow as they entered the hospital. They strolled by the receptionist's desk, and Claudia saw Dr/

Roberts standing in the foyer. She shook her hat. "Hi there. We came in to get her stitches out. Today is all right, isn't it?"

The police rose from behind the counter and came out from the doorway. Claudia ducked, pushing her patient down to the floor. "Is it a shooting? Did a loony get loose?"

Instead of any answers, the police grabbed Claudia, saying, "Claudia Bronk, get your hands up in the air."

"What the!" Claudia exclaimed.

She was cuffed. Claudia was read her rights.

Claudia graveled. "What the Sam Hill do you think you're doing?"

"Here she is, the missing woman. It's Sara." Dr. Roberts thundered.

"Claudia?" Sara felt faint.

Dr. Roberts came over to Claudia. "What were you thinking taking her? We'll deal with you later."

The police nudged Claudia to follow them.

She sidestepped them. "You listen here now, Dr. Roberts!" Claudia belted out in a gruff voice.

Sara raised her hands and closed her eyes. The room was quiet. Sara took a peek.

"Did the night guard give you my papers?" Claudia asked the doctor.

Dr. Roberts raised his eyebrows. "What papers?"

Claudia sighed. "Get the old coot. He had my leave of absence papers and the home care forms signed for Sara's care." She stomped her feet. "Get me out of these cuffs now."

Dr. Roberts threw his hand up in the air. "Stop. Let's get the guard down here."

Claudia was placed on a bench. Sara scooted over to Claudia's feet.

"Hi, Claudia." The old guard slipped his hand in his jacket pocket. "Dr. Roberts, I understand you wanted to see me? Oops. Here's Claudia's paperwork. She wanted me to turn these in to you, Dr. Roberts."

Claudia heard, "Uncuff her." She whirled and stomped over to the night guard. She took her finger and pointed it in his face. She saw how broken he looked. She rubbed her wrists and took a step backward, grumbling. "Thank you for remembering my request now."

Claudia quickly looked at the woman with the lost memory, now trying to stand and was shaking. *She looked like a deer facing the headlights, wanting to run.*

Claudia went to her and clasped her arms around her. "Dr. Roberts has found your name." Looking into the woman's eyes, she said, "Baby girl, it's Sara."

Tears formed in her eyes as she said, "My name is Sara?"

Claudia looked around the area. The police were gone. They had disappeared as quickly as they had arrived. Dr. Roberts pulled the security guard into the office, and his voice was not calm. He came out from the room, and Claudia—with Sara—saw him having his shoulders a little more drooped.

As he left through the big doors, he stopped and glanced over his right shoulder. "I'm sorry, Claudia. I didn't mean to cause you or her any harm."

Claudia sighed and picked up the security guard, giving him a bear hug. "You old goat, anyhow."

Dr. Roberts immediately held a press conference proudly announcing Sara's return. He answered questions and had asked Sara not to speak. Claudia stood close by as a protective mother hen. As the press left, Sara gave a shy wave and turned, joining Claudia in the doctor's office.

Mr. Life was waiting. He removed the stitches. He found Sara's memory had improved a little. He had tests run and studied her charts. She could answer some questions but didn't remember how she knew the answers.

The doctor spoke with Claudia. "Most of her swelling has subsided. Will Sara be staying with you?"

"Yes, for a while longer," Claudia answered.

Sara was nodding as she fingered her necklace.

They walked out, and Sara jumped up into the truck. She was quiet on the way to Claudia's farm. Claudia served them a hot cup of tea and encouraged Sara to lie down.

Stilled unnerved by the day's happenings, Claudia took a deep breath and went for a long hard horse ride. The winds pounded at her face and edged her farther. She had let the rage out and settled the fearlessness of herself.

The ride to the barn seemed endless. Every joint in her body ached. She climbed the back steps and checked on Sara before heading to the shower. As the water poured over her shoulders, she stretched, welcoming its warmth. She toweled and had just finished snapping her bibs when the back doorbell dinged, followed by a knock. She took the stairs two at a time, hoping the sound would not awaken Sara.

As the door stood ajar, it revealed two men. Claudia wondered what this place was getting to be. Instead of quietness and being a serene dwelling, it had become like a Grand Central Station.

Claudia stood behind the screen and eyed the men. They wore suits. "Didn't you see the 'Do not trespass' sign? State your business and be gone with yourself." She reached for a baseball bat.

Donald stepped backward. Weakly, he introduced them. "My name is Donald, and this is Jack. We understand Sara News is here. Dr. Roberts met with us today right after the news conference. We just missed you both." He glanced across at the surprisingly wide-eyed woman and then at Jack.

The woman stuttered. "I'm Claudia Bronks, Sara's nurse. She's resting. Who are you to her, and what do you want?"

Donald spoke. "Please put down the bat. I'm a friend of Sara and her husband."

Jack stretched his hand and offered it to Claudia. She stepped from behind the screen door, and had a twisted smile. She shook his hand. "So who is whom to Sara?"

Jack had left his hand lingering in hers longer than needed. "Sara was in my Wednesday-night study group. I'm a good friend."

Donald regained his composure. "We would like to see Sara. Is that possible?"

"Come sit a spell," Claudia said. "You do know Sara has suffered most memory loss. I doubt she will remember either of you. If one of you has the time and want to stay here after the introductions are made, I can fix you up in the bunkhouse." She shook her head. "Having both of you stay would be too much for her, in Sara's fragile state." She stood up. "Would you like a glass of ice tea or lemonade?"

Both men were in unison when they answered, "Tea's fine."

Taking a sip, Donald forced his tea down. He looked at Jack, but his eyes were locked with Claudia's. Donald went ahead speaking. "Are you okay with staying here at Mrs. Bronks, without me?"

Claudia jerked. It's miss."

Donald touched Jack's shoulder. "I can inform the families involved and give them an update about Sara and her whereabouts. Jack, Jack?"

"What?" Jack said. "Yes, staying here. I'm fine."

Donald slipped a chuckle, and was amused with Jack, given these circumstances.

Just then Sara came out on the porch, carrying some sandwiches and a pitcher of ice tea. She turned pink. "Hello, am I interrupting? Are you here inquiring about the purchase of a horse?" She smiled.

Claudia spoke. "Thanks for the refreshments. Now sit down, child. These men came by to see and visit with you."

Sara's drink went up in the air, then she cried. "Do I know them? I don't recognize either of them. I'm hopeless!"

Jack reached out and touched Sara's cheek. "It's okay. Your memory will come back in time. You need more rest to heal. My name is Jack. Claudia said I could stay in the bunkhouse for a few days. If it is all right, we could visit and get reacquainted. How do you feel about my staying, Sara?"

Claudia handed Sara a damp rag and poured her another glass of tea. "Now, now, it's all right." She held Sara in her strong arms.

Sara whimpered, peeking under Claudia's arm. "It's fine if you stay, Jack. Claudia, I'm going to lie back down."

She stood up and left the room. The door closed behind her, and Claudia called Donald a cab.

Donald thanked Claudia for her time and let her know he appreciated the care and help she was giving Sara. "You have my number. Call me." He reached inside a pocket and pulled out a pad and pen. "Claudia, may I have your phone number? Sara's husband, I'm sure, will call."

Donald watched from the back window of the cab until his friends and the farm was out of sight. He had a layover at the airport. He loosened his tie.

It was an unusually hot, hot, hot day. On the plane, he shucked his jacket and opened the top of his shirt. Upon arriving, he found the weather was still balmy. Donald rolled up his sleeves as he walked to the cab station.

He would soon be home, and that was good. Upon arriving, he took a deep breath and entered by the apartment entrance. As he looked around, he realized it was great he had avoided everyone.

Donald needed a shower in the worst way. Standing and letting the water flow over him was fantastic. He finally washed the sweat and dust off. He reached into the closet and got himself a casual pair of slacks and a crisp white shirt. He dabbed a little aftershave on and once again rolled up his sleeves. He heard the suit's door open and quick soft steps entering the room.

He let out a sigh. "Kate, is that you? I've missed you. Come here." He swung her around and gave her a hug. "Were you fixing dinner? I'm starved."

Kate took his hand. "Let's go to the kitchen." She embraced him again and felt the tension in his arms. His eyes looked glazed.

Sitting at the table, he forced himself to eat. Kate's cooking was great. His mouth still full, he said, "Thank you, Kate."

"Hi, Dad. When did you get in?" asked Karen.

Donald smiled. "Not long ago, Karen, Jud. Well, hello, Luci, Luke."

"Grandpa, we're going swimming. The new guard is downstairs. You coming?" Luke asked.

"Not this time, sport. I need to make a few calls and then sit down with your mother and father." Donald looked at Kate. She was beaming with her arms crossed. She gave him a wink and kept on working in the kitchen.

Donald carried a mug of coffee with him into the parlor. Jud had placed his cup down, and Karen held an ice tea.

Karen and Jud waited on the love seat as Donald paced back and forth. He took a sip. "Karen, Jud, we found Sara. The hospital held a press meeting and explained everything. The TV channel should be doing a feature story about Sara. It seems there was a mix-up from the beginning in the communications and signed paperwork. Sara was and is staying with a nurse. Her name is Claudia Bronk."

Setting his mug down, he went on, "She's a sight. The nurse, that is. Claudia is a stout and strong person. She's single and owns on a horse farm in Kentucky. She has strange colors in her flyaway curly hair, and it is long." Donald sighed. "Sara appears healthy but is still suffering from memory loss. I was a complete stranger to her."

"Dad, did she have on the penny swear necklace?" Karen asked.

"Yes, Karen, she did. Matter of fact, she was toying with it when I left Jack."

Jud spoke up. "What's Jack doing there? Although I think Mr. Nite being there is a good thing. You know his voice is soft, and Sara always enjoyed his classes." He took another refill. "Claudia seemed to be awestruck by Jack, and I think he liked her too." Donald added.

He stroked his chin. "This could be interesting."

"Enough talking tonight, Donald," Kate said. "You can finish your conversation tomorrow." She placed her hand in his. "Good night, Karen, Jud." She gave that look and turned to Donald. Never letting go of his hand, she took her head and motioned toward the stairs.

He let her lead. His jaw dropped. She pulled back the sheets and took off his shoes and socks. She handed him his pajama bottoms. She turned out the light and nudged the door.

"Lie with me, Kate."

The bed squeaked.

The moonlight drifted as a new day on the horizon streamed through the window. Donald placed his hands across his eyes. He reached for Kate, but only her impression was left. He padded to the shower, and showered cold. He dressed and headed downstairs to face more questions from Jud and Karen.

He waved breakfast away. He picked up coffee and a slice of toast, and pointed to the other room. "Ask away. Oh, I have Claudia's number." He smiled. "Karen, you can call Sara's nurse in a couple of days, and maybe make arrangements to see her." He chuckled as he looked at his daughter. "Beware. Claudia is different, but she seems to know her business."

Donald took another piece of toast. "Jud, since the bank meeting is held at Ken's, do you want to take this number with you, or do you want me to call him?"

13

Donald used the phone to call Ken. He stretched, and realized the strain in his neck had almost disappeared.

"Hello? Ken, I'm glad I caught you in. This is Donald, and I have some good news. Sara is found and has been presented with her name. She is staying with her nurse Claudia, and Jack is there trying to help. Unfortunately, Sara didn't recognize him either. Here is the nurse's number so you can make contact."

Ken let out a long sigh. "I'm thankful she's alive." He clasped his hands. "Thank you for caring about our family and your loyalty, Donald. I'll let Louise know. Sir, does Sara have any memory of what has happened? Does she know anyone yet?"

"Sorry, Ken, she doesn't recall much. Give it time."

"Thanks for the update and the phone number." Ken paused. "All I have is time. I love her so."

"Pray, Ken," Donald advised. "He hears and answers. Give my regards to all. Bye now."

"Bye."

Donald heard Jud's coins jingle as he joined him.

"Sir, I personally want to thank you for the way you managed this massive mess and rose to the responsibility about Sara," Jud said. "I understand the value of a person. I have truly learned from your example on how to be there for others. Thank you for that, Donald."

"Well, we are to follow His example. He will guide." Donald began chuckling. "What's that all about?"

"Tell you the truth, I was thinking about Jack."

Another chuckle escaped as Donald hit his knee. "Jack appeared awestruck with Sara's nurse. He stuttered when he tried to talk with her, and he held her hand longer than a necessary shake. Jack was led around by Claudia. I never would have guessed it of Jack."

Jud shook his head and snickered. "Wonder how things will go between Sara, Claudia, and Jack. Oh my."

Donald stood and crossed the room. "Jud, how did Spencer make out about the land contract case?"

Jud took a deep breath. "Spencer was great, Donald. He convinced the judge of the bank's right and how insufferable it would be at this time to change the law. The judge went over the land contract and picked it apart, but Spencer was shrewd. He never lost focus, and he had the land contractor on the stand admitting everything had been explained, and a forty-eight-hour change-of-mind clause was also included for the customers' own protection. He even stated that a lawyer was present to offer advice should he have any questions and that he wavered it of his own free will."

"Jud, I have to agree, Spencer is superb," Donald said. "His expenses are costly, but his results are excellent. Well." He patted Jud on the back. "I'm glad everything has worked out for you at the bank and for the other branches."

Jud shifted. "I know when you spoke with your dad he must have been thrilled. I remember Tom in those days and his ways. He was a force to be reckoned with. Like father, like son."

"Mom, can you take care of Luke and Luci today?" Karen asked.

"Sure. What's up?"

"I talked with Claudia and booked a flight for there today. She stated I could come for a two-hour visit. She felt it might even help Sara." Karen tapped her chin. "I have to try, Mom."

"I know. Be sure and pray Karen, and don't be disappointed. These things take time. It's in His time, remember."

Karen's nerves flip-flopped in her stomach. As she reached the front porch, she was greeted by this woman, Nurse Claudia. Karen couldn't help but gasp and stare. She tried looking in a different direction, but Claudia was in bibs showing lumps and shapelessness. Her features were hard, and her hands felt like leather. A thought popped into her head: Was she really a nurse?

A boisterous voice came out of Claudia. "Sit here." She patted a wooden chair. Karen saw Jack stepped up and stood by the rail. He was so lean and clean-shaven. His muscles were small but firm.

Softly, he spoke. "Good seeing you, Karen." He tipped his hat at Claudia. Karen saw him blush. *He likes Claudia.*

Karen turned and caught sight of Claudia's mouth become soft with a slim smile. *Claudia likes him.*

Karen bit her lip, trying not to laugh. Who would have thought Jack the study teacher would be smitten?

Sara came out the door and went over to Claudia. She seemed codependent on her. Karen touched her necklace, and noticed Sara had too. "Hi, Sara, my name is Karen Day. I see you have a necklace like mine."

Sara offered her hand to Karen and scooted back. "Have we met before?"

Karen moved a little forward with a thin smile. "Yes, we have met. Matter of fact, we are best friends."

Karen saw Sara's eyes narrow. "Now don't worry, Sara," Karen said hurriedly. "Your memory will all come back in good time."

"I like your purse, Karen," Sara said. "It looks roomy."

"Sara, I brought you a purse," Karen said. "It's almost like mine. See, I made it. You taught me how."

Sara reached for her head. "Claudia, help me."

"Jack, get a cool cloth, please," Claudia instructed.

"Here you are," Jack said. "Is it wrung out enough?"

Their fingers touched. A big smile lit up Jack's face as he lowered himself into the double wide chair. He sat across from Sara.

"Karen." Sara looked from under Claudia's arm, reaching to take Karen's hand in hers. "Your husband's name is Jud, and he is a ruggedly handsome man. Women ogle him. Right?"

Karen rushed to Sara's side and hugged her. "You are so right. He's a looker and a real charmer."

"Claudia, this is the woman I told you about that had the necklace like mine," Sara said. "See? She does."

Claudia stopped the rocker. "Who's in the cab, or is it for you, Karen?"

Karen whistled and motioned for the driver to stay. "It's been very nice to see you, Sara. I'm praying for you, and I love you. Your memory is improving, and all will come back. You're doing great. Have Claudia dial me sometime if you want to talk."

Sara squeezed Karen's hand and waved good-bye. Sara watched as the cab left but locked eyes on a tall dark-haired dimpled man. His skin made Sara want to touch him. She blinked.

Ken slipped but kept his balance. "Thank you, Miss Claudia, for allowing me to come to your farm. It's quite impressive."

Sara watched as Claudia thrust her hand forward.

"You are Ken?" Claudia asked.

"I am."

"Pleased to meet you then. Jack, show him to the bunkhouse. Be back here, both of you, by 6:00 p.m. sharp. Come, Sara, we'll fix dinner."

Sara twisted her head, stood, and gawked with uncertainty. The man turned, showing a wide chesty smile. She found herself drawn to him, and his eyes seemed familiar. Boldly, Sara waved just before darting into the house.

Claudia had Sara peel potatoes while she stepped out to the bunk area. She rapped on the door. "Mr. News, I would like a word with you."

Ken looked upon Claudia from behind the screen door. "Yes." An eyebrow rose. He had been watching the house and saw Sara moved the pan of potatoes from the sink to the window so she could watch. Sara stretched and slightly opened the window to hear what may be spoken.

Ken extended his head out the door, not sure if he needed to duck. "Yes? What is it, ma'am?"

Claudia had fisted hands on her hips. "I trust your stay here will benefit all of us. Sara remembers very little about the past, and she doesn't remember anything about a husband. You must approach her as if you're meeting her for the first time. You're beginning over. You are a complete stranger to her although I think there's a spark. Remember, if you upset Sara in any way, you are out of here. Do you understand?"

Sara cringed. She saw Ken flinch, and Jack put a hand on his shoulder.

"Answer me," Claudia bellowed once again. "Do you understand my rules?"

Ken backed up even more. He could only nod. Sara quickly moved from the window so Claudia would not know she was watching or listening. Sara tilted her head. *Could he be my husband?* Sara wiped her hands. *He's so good-looking.*

Jack welcomed Ken. "I'm glad you're here. Sara needs you."

Ken's eyebrows were next to his hairline.

"Oh, Claudia is a sweet one," Jack assured Ken. "She just wants what's best for her patient."

Shrugging, Ken began to unpack. Jack showed him his two drawers and helped him hang his shirts. "Come on. I'll show you around first then you can shower. It will refresh you."

As they walked side by side, Jack easily mentioned, "Ken, do approach Sara with kindness and show her tenderness. Go slowly and take your time. You need to rebuild a relationship. Sara will want to get acquainted, but she's scared and confused, not knowing if you are anyone important in her life or could be and wondering if she can trust you. It's a lot for her to deal with. Be strong, and don't expect too much so soon."

"Thanks, Jack." Ken stretched. "Claudia has a real nice spread. Look at those horses."

"Yes, she does, and Claudia has had a hard life." As they walked back to the bunkhouse, Jack said, "I'll hop in the shower and be out in ten minutes."

Ken sat on the bunk bed, taking off his boots.

Jack came out of the shower. "Your turn, Ken."

Ken grabbed his clothes to change. He reached for the nozzle to turn on the water and for a brief moment forgot where he was.

"Hurry up, Ken," Jack called out. "We have to be at the house in thirty minutes."

Ken dropped the soap, and knots formed in his stomach. He finished with shaving and slapped on some musk-scented aftershave. He tried on his shirt and jeans, and none suited him. "Jack, how formal is this dinner?"

"It isn't. Claudia is common."

Ken decided on a fitted blue pullover instead and tucked the tail in his jeans. He took the tips of his shoes and dusted them off on the back of the jean legs. "What do you think, Jack? How do I look?"

"You'll do," Jack answered. "If you wait any longer, Ken, it won't matter what you're wearing, for we will be turned away from dinner. One thing for Claudia, she is punctual."

Ken glanced at Jack and saw he was headed out the door. "I'm coming, Jack. I'm as nervous as a chicken with its head cut off about being around Sara. My palms are even sweaty. I don't remember being this scared when we first met."

"You'll be all right. Just calm down and breathe deeply. Exhale slowly."

"Jack, you've gotten quiet," Ken observed. "Is something wrong?"

"No," Jack said. "It's just my stomach is a little unsettled when I go near Claudia."

"Do you have feelings for her, Mr. Nite?"

Jack's neck and face were turning red.

Jack nodded. "Yes."

They stepped on the front porch where Sara stood opening the door. Ken reached over for Jack's shoulder. His knees were buckling. Jack's eyes grew narrow, and Ken willed himself to say, "Hello, Sara. I'm Ken."

As he walked by her, a whiff of her floral cologne crossed his nose. He could only squeak out a hello to Claudia. Dinner went well, and Jack talked with Sara mostly.

Claudia played some easy listening music. She held out her hand and bowed to Ken. He bowed back and felt like a klutz, having Claudia in his arms. The song ended, but not too soon for Ken. He thought Claudia had four feet, for they were all over his.

"Ken, switch partners." He slowly swung Sara around. Ken felt his mouth open wide as Sara took his hand and took two steps. He hadn't moved.

She stopped. "Well?"

Ken gasped. "Sorry. Sara, shall we?"

Again they were on the floor, swaying to the music. She felt right, good in his arms. She leaned in closer. He slowed his steps, and she followed. Ken glanced over at Jack. He was counting the beat and swinging Claudia and stepping out of the rhythm, but Claudia didn't seem to notice. She swung her arms up and down right along with Jack. A chuckle rolled out. *What a sight.*

Sara looked up at his laughter. She flashed a flirty smile and placed her arms around his neck and slowed her steps, and made proper conversation. The music stopped, and Sara pulled at his ponytail and ran from the room.

Claudia's eyebrows stretched together. "Ken, it's time you head for the bunkhouse."

Ken nodded and looked over to Jack, but he was deeply looking into Claudia's eyes.

"Jack, can you stay awhile?" Claudia asked.

Ken kicked at a stone lying in the driveway, as he walked back to the bunkhouse. He glanced out the side window and caught Sara staring back, and he waved. He grabbed his T-shirt and cleared the window some, but Sara was gone.

Undressing for bed, he thought. Had they made a connection? Did she feel attraction for him as he did for her? His stomach rolled, and his knees were weak. Ken was driven to his knees. He bowed his head and clasped his hands. He uttered, "Help me, and help *us*."

Lying in bed, he stared at the ceiling. He felt somewhat comforted. Ken knew he would see Sara again tomorrow, for they had scheduled a board game even if it was with Claudia and Jack.

Ken turned on his side and then his back. Sleep was not happening. He fluffed up his pillow. The door cracked, and Jack stepped in. Ken shivered and asked, "Did Sara mention anything about me?" He sat up on the side of his bed waiting. "Jack, Jack?" He listened, but only snoring filled the air. Jack still had his shoes on.

The next morning, when the sun was barely up, Jack shook Ken. "Come on, we're going into town for Claudia."

"What?" Ken asked.

"We're hauling feed for Claudia's horses."

Ken had a five-minute shower and headed after Jack to the house, buttoning his shirt. He sat, prayed, and ate pancakes and eggs.

"Claudia, thanks for breakfast. The coffee is real good." Ken rocked back on his boots. "Claudia, may I use your phone for a business call? I'll pay."

Claudia wiped her hands on the sagging apron. "Be sure to leave the money for your phone call on the counter."

Ken reached in his jeans pocket and pulled out two dollars and thirty-five cents for the call. "Hello, J. J.? I made it to Claudia's farm. She has a huge spread and exquisite horses. Some of the best breeds around."

"Maybe you can work out a horse deal," J. J. suggested. "That's wonderful. Did you see Sara?"

"I did. We met, but I'm not sure her memory was jogged." Ken took a sip of coffee. He sighed. "Here's hoping."

"You need to romance her and bring her home like a bride." J. J. chuckled. "Ken, I had a surprise visit from my sister today. She's staying until next month's meeting. She knows this bank business inside and out and has offered to help. She even has a few suggestions for you."

"I know her reputation for—business. It precedes her. Check to see what her ideas are, and if it should be smoothly implemented. How's the boys, and Louise, Mom, and Dad?"

"Everything and everyone here is fine. Sam is helping Louise out with Matthew and Timmy, although I don't think she needs any help. Here's sis. I have to go." J. J. was hanging up, and Ken heard, "Coming."

Ken was amused. *J. J. would make a fine banker someday. Soon, maybe. He just needed to stay focused.*

Ken reached into his pocket for more change, adding to the amount on the counter. He dialed another number.

"Jud," Ken spoke. "It's good to hear your voice."

"I'm so sorry I haven't been there for you, friend," Jud said.

"Jud, I understand. We'll get caught up on banking next month at our meeting. Sorry the other meeting was canceled, but this call is about Sara. I'm here at Claudia's farm. Jud, my feelings for Sara are pinned inside me. Knowing I cannot express them is killing me."

"Ken, it's going to be all right. You both were brought together once. Things have a way of working themselves out. It does take time. You need to woo her. You haven't forgotten how, have you?"

Ken let out a long breath. "Funny, friend. I know. I'm nervous though. Thanks for listening and for praying."

"Ken, move slowly," Jud advised. "Show Sara around, have a picnic, go for a ride. Compliment her, and pick her flowers. Did you bring any pictures with you? Ask Sara if see would like to see them."

"Thanks again, Jud. Oh, Jack said hi, and is poking me on my back. Bye, friend."

Ken straightened and adjusted his emotions. He gave himself a talking-to. *Dating it is. I must win her back.*

Ken and Sara played board games, took walks, and cared for the animals. They even planned rides. Two weeks fled by. They were allotted more and more time alone. Ken was relaxed around Sara, and only became tense around Claudia.

One month passed. Things seemed smoother between Sara and him. He was looking forward to the ride and picnic they had planned for today. He checked to see if he had the pictures. After looking, he slipped them into his saddlebag, slung a blanket, and helped Sara onto her horse. He rode with the picnic basket in hand.

Ken felt energized and hoped Sara would soon have a breakthrough of her past. Thoughts were running across his mind. *Go slowly. Sara's a gifted rider. Show her around. Go slowly with her feelings.*

He glanced her way. "What?"

Sara had a flirty smile, "Let's race."

"You sure?" Ken asked. "I think we ought to just trot or walk."

Her shirttail was flying from behind. He kicked the sides of his horse and galloped after Sara. He arrived, and she was tapping her foot. "What took you so long?" She laughed.

Ken's smiled broadened. He dropped the basket, took the blanket from the horse, and reached for the pictures.

Conversation flowed. Sara's shoulders seemed relaxed. They ate fried chicken, and he commented on Sara's cooking as he wiped his mouth. She, with napkin in hand, touched the side of his lips. Ken trembled but smiled. He reached for the pictures. "Want to see?"

She observed the first photo. "Is this your farm? I like the porch. So inviting."

He nodded as he handed her the second picture.

"The boys look like mini me's of you, Ken."

He laughed. Tapping his chin, he saw the reflection of himself. He offered her the rest of the pictures, and said, "Are you recalling anything?"

She shook her head as a tear fell. Ken's knuckles lightly grazed her cheek. She was so close he felt her breath and smelled the chicken. He saw warmth in her eyes. He bent and lightly brushed her lips. Her eyes widened, and his stomach felt toyed.

"Ken." Sara put her fists to his shoulders and cleared her throat. "I want you to know that I overheard Claudia speaking with you and Jack the day you arrived. She told you both not to mention that you are…my husband."

14

Ken, overjoyed, pulled Sara closer. He bent his head and passionately kissed her.

She pulled back and gave him a slap. "Listen. I overheard the word *husband*, not that I *know* you are my husband." Although she looked through long lashes while she licked her lips, a smile surrounded the corners of her mouth. "Cowboy, you can surely kiss." She quickly hoisted herself up mounting on the horse and left Ken behind.

He arrived at the barn as she alit from the horse. Sara began rubbing the mare down. Ken stood next to her, doing the same thing. His eyes seemed smokily wicked. She kept silent but shyly smiled.

Claudia came from the barn and motioned to Jack. "Sara, Ken, how was your ride?"

Sara felt color rising from her neck to her face. "It was an eye-opener, and I learned a lot today." She glanced Ken's way, and walked to where he stood. Sara, on tiptoes, leaned onto him and touched his shoulder, whispering, "Want to walk with me?"

He stuttered, "S-s-sure." His breathing was still raspy.

Sara took his hand. He looked straight ahead. "When you touch me, I feel like a hot coal has touched my chest. Sara, don't you feel my love for you? Can you trust me?"

She glanced at him and smiled. "Cowboy, maybe you ought to try another kiss."

His eyes darkened more. He tried to speak but was tongue-tied.

"Oh, for heaven's sake." She put her arms around his neck and saw him blush. She tickled the back of his neck and pulled his ponytail.

He tipped his hat and took a long look before gently brushing her lips. He moved sideways. She clung to and stepped with him. She kissed him back. He swept her up and swung her around. "I love you, Sara. I always have, and I always will." His kiss deepened.

"Put me down, Ken." Sara was shaking.

His eyes flew opened and widened. He was puzzled, but obeyed. "Sara," he gasped.

She crossed her arms to her chest. "Ken, I know mentally who you really are, but to me, I'm just not ready yet. My life is so unsettling. I'm trying, and you are very tempting. Did we get along before?"

He dragged his toe. "Sara, are you ready to go home with me? You can trust me—always. Have faith. Please?"

"Let's wait another week here. I'll see the doctor again with Claudia and decide from there."

He touched her shoulder. "All right, I'll do things your way for now, but it's hard."

Four days passed. The day was sunny with a slight chill. Sara was released from the doctors, and Claudia fixed a feast to celebrate. It was self-serve night. Claudia cranked up the music. Jack took Claudia's hand and swung less. He dance a little slower, and Jack stole a kiss.

Claudia had to fan herself.

Ken did a variety of dancing with Sara. A waltz came on, and he bowed. She curtsied. They danced to a few bars. Sara dropped her hold and took his hand and began walking toward the door. They walked out to the barn.

"I need a kiss," Sara said.

This time, there was no hesitation. Ken pulled her to him and parted her lips. She squirmed. He held her tighter and kissed her more passionately. She broke loose and gave him a blazing stare before running toward the house. He rushed to stop her and grabbed her arm. She yelled.

"Wait, Sara! What's wrong?"

She stepped on his foot and distanced herself.

Claudia stepped on Sara's path and held out her arms. "Oh, baby girl, what happened?"

Ken stood there—slumped, condemned, and doomed.

Jack ran to Ken. "What happened?"

Ken lowered his head then straightened and locked eyes with Jack. "I kissed her, and she was kissing me back. It felt right, and I made another move. She bolted, and here we are. Jack, the stare she gave me was cold. It chilled me to the bone. I think it best if I leave tonight, before Claudia throws me off the farm."

Jack patted Ken on the back and scratched his chin. "It sure is hard to figure out when a woman wants you to make a move, isn't it?" He shook his head. "Look, Claudia is walking Sara into the house. Want to come in and at least eat?"

"No," Ken said. "You go on ahead. I'm going to stay out in the bunkhouse and write Sara a note. I don't think she wants me here. She needs time, and our boys need at least one parent at home. Jack, will you call me a cab and give Sara my letter?"

Dear Sara,

I wish I could make life better for you. I'm sorry for the pain I have brought you. I love you, and I'm going back to the farm and take care of your mother and our boys. I hope you will want a married life with me someday. I'll wait and pray. Bye for now, my sweet, sweet Sara.

Love always,
Ken

◇◇◇◇◇◇◇◇◇◇

The moon was bright and mostly full, but hearing Claudia approaching the bunkhouse caused despair and gloom. She knocked on the door. Jack slipped in behind her.

"Ken, I know Sara feels something for you, but you crossed the line. You knew the rules. I'm sorry, but you have to leave." Turning, Claudia said, "You can call me and see how Sara is doing from time to time." She moved forward. "That's the best I can do for you. Good-bye and good luck. Sorry, Ken." Claudia wheeled around. "Jack, call Ken a cab. Now!"

"I did, Claudia. Ken already asked me to. Claudia, don't keep your lovely feathers ruffled."

Ken's jaw dropped. His shoulders slumped. He placed his hat lower on his head to shield his eyes.

Jack came and stood with him with hands in his pockets. "I'm so sorry, Ken."

"Jack, I feel like I was just summoned to the principal's office. I feel guilty, like I had been caught stealing candy. Jack, all we did was kiss." Ken hit the door. "She's my wife!"

Jack shuffled his hat and shook his head.

"The boys need stability in their life, so it's best I leave," Ken went on. "At least I will always remember the kiss." He hung his head. "Bye, Jack."

Jack hugged Ken before watching him get into the cab. He handed Ken his luggage.

Claudia shook her head. "I'm sorry it didn't work out, Ken. What a crying shame."

Ken waved. He glanced one last time to window where he once saw Sara. The light was on, but there was no sign of her. He closed the cab door rolled the window partly down and motioned for the driver to leave.

The back screen door banged open.

"Ken, Ken!"

He heard a sound, and glanced backward. Sara was running and yelling. He stopped the cab and opened the door.

"Ken, don't go," Sara said. "Take me with you. I need to see Timmy and Matthew."

He placed his hands on his hips. "You sure this time?"

Claudia stepped closer. "Sara, be sure."

Nodding, Sara shook Claudia's hand and smiled. "Thanks is such a small word for all you've done for me." Turning, she looked at Ken. "I love you. I remembered everything." She fingered her necklace. "The plane, Karen, my business, and you coming to Ohio to surprise me. And, oh, yes, my mom. She moved to live with us." She took a breath. "Now that was a surprise."

"Sara, I didn't see that coming either, but you know I love your mother," Ken said.

She clung onto Ken's shirt. "I'm sorry I hurt you, but you are so charming."

Claudia checked with Sara to make sure she was all right, and she nodded to Ken. "Take good care of Baby Girl."

Jack wiped at his tears and handed Claudia his handkerchief. She blew, and there was a loud sound.

Jack placed an arm around Claudia and gave her a squeeze.

She looked up to him. "You big oaf." She reached for Jack's ear and pulled him nearer.

The cab driver waited for Sara to get in.

"Claudia, send me my luggage, and call," Sara said. "Thank you for everything. I love you."

Jon was busy working on the new addition. He found himself really enjoying the pounding and sawing work and the smell of wood. It was a nice break from farming. Standing back with his hands on his hips, he admired the rooms. He heard Sylvia's and Louise footsteps and he turned.

"We wanted to see what all the pounding is about."

Jon folded his arms. "Louise, Sylvia, what do you think Sara will say about her new business space? Ken did swell drawing up the plans, and he was right on the money with the lumber."

"Jon, Sara will really appreciate all the hard work. It's beautiful." Sylvia joined her husband. "I am so proud of you. All those long hours you have labored." She clasped her hands. "Thanks for working without Ken. It means a lot to me—him."

Jon slipped his hands in his pockets and shrugged. "The work should be completed by tomorrow. No later than this weekend. Let's celebrate." He found himself laughing and the house echoing him. "I'll pay. Does anyone deliver pizza way out here?"

Ken directed the cab driver to a car rental place. After talking with Sara, he decided traveling home in a vehicle was better than flying to the farm. This would be a new adventure.

Ken either had his arm around Sara's shoulder, or on her knee, or was holding her hand. He constantly spoke his quest of his undying love and tried to explain its depth.

He slowed the car down and placed it on cruise so they could enjoy a pleasurable drive home. He wanted for them to talk and get reacquainted. They were together, and he had all the time in the world.

Sara squeezed his arm and gave Ken a quick peck. Both seemed relaxed. They smiled and giggled and sang songs.

The day was threatening a heat wave for the time of the year. According to the radio, it would beat any former record. Ken pulled over and rolled both back windows down. He reached for the basket. "Sara, Claudia packed us a lunch and a supper, it looks like. Would you like for us to take a break to stretch and then eat?"

She locked eyes with him, and he saw vulnerability. She gave a faint nod, took her sweater, and slipped it on. "You carry the blanket, and I've got the basket."

There was only wheat all around them. It was breathtaking. The blanket was fluffed out, and they sat down.

"You want peanut-butter with grape jelly or peach, Sara?"

"Peach sounds good." She smiled and touched his hand. "Ken, look at the pen-shaped blue spruce trees in their clustered rows. They seemed to be giving me a hearty 'Welcome back home.'"

They briefly touched lips. Ken shivered, and Sara gasped.

"Ken, look out over the wheat fields."

He cupped his hand over his brow. "Yes, the wheat is almost ready to harvest."

"Oh, Ken, they are much more than food for a harvest. Really see. It's their tops. They look like there is a little hat sitting on their shafts." Sara rose and twirled. "See the glistening in the fields. It's as if the tassels were dripping pure gold."

Ken tilted his hat back. He viewed the sights through different thought lenses. He pointed out the man-made ponds.

"They are fine-looking, and to think they are replenished each year with bass, bluegill, and catfish." She twirled and laughed some more.

Ken gazed at Sara's hair. She had insisted it all be shaved. He marveled at her strength and inner beauty. She now had almost two months' hair growth, and her head was shaped perfectly.

Sara spread her arms open wide. "There are miles and miles of land, and yet it holds everything of His creation. It's reassuring to know He's everywhere, and that He goes with you, and He knows all."

Ken was overwhelmed by Sara. He moved closer and swung her around. Their lips touched, and he intensified his hold. He lavished in sprinkling soft kisses on her cheeks. They talked, and he laid her on the blanket, snuggling closer. He held on to her for dear life. She yawned. Ken was content to just hold her, and they slept.

Ken gradually opened his eyes and saw the birds flying toward the trees. He carefully moved, not wanting to wake Sara. He stretched and reached for some water from the basket. He munched on another sandwich and felt a drop of rain. He held his hand out, and another drop hit.

He gently shook Sara, and still another drop of rain fell. She sprung up. She grabbed the basket and he the blanket, and they trotted to the car. They were like sweethearts who had been caught, and they exploded with laughter. The sky threatened a real downpour.

Ken pulled Sara close. "I hope this storm blows over. If not, it will be rough traveling."

The side of her mouth lifted in a smile. "Let's pray before we journey any further." She kissed him behind the ear and pulled at his ponytail. "Let's wait the storm out. We are safe here, aren't we?"

"You temptress you."

They kissed and kissed.

"Sara, we don't know if this storm will pass," Ken said. "So as much as I would love to stay, we ought to keep driving."

"Okay, cowboy, take me home." Her eyes became vulnerable.

Ken cleared his throat. "Sara, you awaken everything in me. I'm weakening. You sure you don't want to try out the backseat?"

Sara motioned forward and was still laughing as he put the car in drive. They were a long ways down the road. He became amused looking in the rearview mirror of the small backseat, and began laughing until his sides hurt.

The peanut butter made Ken's mouth dry. "Sara, can you reach the water jug?"

Sara took a glass of water and refilled Ken's. The road was narrow in parts and had big puddles. Ken regripped the steering wheel.

The rain stopped as quickly as it came, and the heat dried the ground. Sara wiped the inside window, brushing the dust that came in.

Ken noticed the flower scent floating under his nose. Sara looked so fresh. He adjusted himself in his seat. This was going to be a long ride home. Good and bad. "What are you looking at, Sara?"

"Just wondering where you went, for there was a faraway look in your eyes."

Ken smiled and turned on the radio. "I'm right here with you, darling." He patted the seat. Sara snuggled closer, and he let out a long breath and whistled.

Ken drove well into the night. The moon was big and orange. The air was clear, and the stars twinkled. He saw Sara shiver, and placed his arm around her. She smiled back as she leaned her head on him, closing her eyes.

He was glad when he pulled off the main highway and onto the concealed gravel lane. He drove a little farther and stopped.

Sara gasped. "Home sweet home." She wrapped her arms around his neck and kissed him. His eyes enlarged. She deepened her lip pressure and pulled at his hair. He undid the hair band, and his hair arrayed around him. Ken made circular motions on her neck, and she responded. He dropped his hat and kissed her neck.

Sara squealed. "Let's get home, Ken." She touched his chest and played with his top shirt button. He gassed the engine and plunged forward. Soon, the car was in the drive. She slipped from the car as he carried in the basket. They moved from the kitchen to the boys' room. She padded her way to check on her mom. She stopped just outside her door and heard her snore. Sara covered her mouth to keep a laugh from escaping.

Ken watched as she moved from room to room. He paused outside their bedroom door. "Want me to sleep in the spare bedroom tonight?" Not waiting for a response, he lifted his hat and turned.

Sara stepped forward and touched his shoulder. She went on her tiptoes, giving him a kiss. She yanked him by the shirttail.

"Sara, are you sure?" Ken asked.

She traced his mouth and waggled her index finger, motioning him inside.

The corners at his mouth lifted, as did his eyebrows. Ken hauled Sara in his arms and pushed the door closed with his foot, carefully placing her on the bed, where he threw his hat. He sat down and pulled off his boots. He turned for a glance at Sara. She gave him a flirty look, and her finger was still waggling.

15

Morning came. Sara stood in the kitchen, rubbing her arms. She stared out the window, seeing nothing. She bowed her head. *Thank you for watching over me on my adventures, and thanks for a second chance in this march of life.*

She measured grounds and placed them in the coffeemaker. It began perking away. She checked the supply cabinet and gathered what was needed to make fresh strawberry pancakes.

She thought the children were so handsome in their sleep. She took a few steps and saw her mom's apron. She clutched it to her chest.

Ken walked to her and held her in his arms. "Hello, beautiful. Welcome home." He placed his chin on her head. "I've missed you."

Sara turned. "And I you."

They kissed.

"Mommy, Mommy. It's me, Timmy."

Tears fell as she reached and pulled him up. "Timmy, I love you, and I have missed you."

Kiss, kiss, kiss.

"Mommy, I was good with Matthew and for Grandma Louise, and I worked with Grandpa Jon too. We—"

"Shush, Timmy. We don't want to spoil the surprise." Sara said.

"Mommy, Mommy, where have you been? I was lonely. No one reads like you do." Matthew was carrying his old raggedy stuffed bear and dropped it to hug Sara's knees.

Louise stepped into the kitchen, waving her hands, and cried, "Lands of mercy. Girl! Come here!"

Sara placed her arms around her mother and whispered, "I love you, Mom. Just hold me. It's nice you are here."

Sniffles were heard throughout the room and some blowing of noses.

"I appreciate you mom more than you will ever know." Sara's eyes were red rimmed.

Sniffling. "I love you too." Sylvia said and she joined Jon, and they entwined their fingers.

"Hello, Sara, welcome back." Jon said.

Tears spilled.

Sara cleared her throat. "It's good to be home."

"How are you?" Jon asked.

"I'm good. The doctors released me and said most of my memory has returned and the rest will come. Thanks for asking."

Jon touched Sara's hand. "I smell pancakes. They aren't burnt, are they?"

Everyone laughed.

Sam rushed in through the back door. "Sara, is that you?"

"Yes, it is," Sara answered. "Come in and sit down, Sam, and have breakfast with us."

Sam smiled as he held the seat for Louise. She sat down, blushing, and he slid onto the bench beside her, reaching for his hat. Turning, he asked, "Did Ken tell you about the new mare, Sara? She's a high jumper."

Ken nodded with a slight smile.

Sara threw her apron down and hastily went outside. Ken hurried and followed.

"What's her name, Ken?" Sara asked.

"She isn't named," Ken answered.

Sam speedily fled to the barn. "She's a beauty, isn't she?"

"Yes, Sam," Sara agreed. "Saddle her up. I'm going for a ride."

"Sara, do you think that's a good idea?"

She placed her hands on her hips. "I do declare, Sam." She turned to Ken. "Ken, her name is Velvety. She's smooth. I'll need to call Claudia." She took the reins and threw her head back. She kicked Velvety's sides, and was off.

Sara felt refreshed as she trotted back to the barn. "Whoa, Velvety."

Sam took the reins.

Sara said, "Thanks, Sam. She's a beauty."

Louise was standing in the doorway, motioning for Sara to come in. "Duck. Don't look under the sheets. Here, take the phone."

"Hello, Claudia?" Sara said. "Wait just a second. There, now it's on speaker. How are you and Jack getting along?"

"He went back to Ohio the next day after you left," Claudia responded. "It's not proper for him to stay here without a chaperone. Sara, he did ask me to come for a visit. But that's not possible."

"Yes, it is," Sara said. "My friend Karen you met, she has a bed-and-breakfast place in Ohio, and it is not very far from Jack's place. Here's her number. Karen will have you chaperone. She'll assign one to you, and she'll keep your courtship proper."

Claudia didn't answer. Sara could only hear her breathe.

Sara let out a breath. "Claudia, one of the horses Ken bought… well, he thinks she's a good one to breed. Would you schedule a time to come here? Maybe we can work out a deal."

"Perhaps," Claudia said. "Sara, I'll get back with you. Can you send me some pictures?"

Sara wanted a glass of ice tea. She found Jon had left a note posted on the refrigerator for her to call Karen. She thought, *Good. I can tell her about Claudia needing a chaperon and that she may call for a room and about Jack. Well, well.*

She could see Jon had checked the sheets to make sure they were still strung across the room area. He had left a Do Not Peek sign pinned and stationed for her eyes.

Sara watched as he entered the work arena. Ken was standing on the heels of his boots with a hammer. He handed his dad a tool belt. They entered, but the sheets were pulled. She would have to wait.

The pounding ceased. The men came to the back area of the door.

"Thanks, Ken, for allowing me to help work with you on this special project," Jon said.

They joked with one another, and Sara noticed Jon and Ken seemed more comfortable around each other. It had taken a long, long time. *Maybe their time apart had eased the tension they shared.*

Sara heard Jon talking, but no one was around. He was praying. *I need to really talk with Ken and let him know how selfish I was trying to keep him on the farm when he had made it clear he wanted a business career in banking. It's not going to be easy.* She shook his head. *You know talking with Ken, but here goes.*

Ken came from the bathroom. "Well, Dad, the last brushstroke of misty green is painted." Completely out of character, he dabbed at his dad with the brush.

Both men burst out loud laughing.

Jon heard Sylvia's light steps. "Can I help? Oh, look at you."

He gave her a squeeze. "Sweetheart, thank you, but you would be in our way right now. How are the grandchildren doing?"

"Oh, they are so wonderful and sweet," Sylvia answered. "We went on walks, and I tried to teach them about Creation along the way. Jon, the bikes that we ordered came in. Louise and I were able to show the boys how to ride. They are so cute."

Jon and Ken walked into the kitchen after they had cleaned up. Louise set lunch in on the table. Sylvia poured the coffee and served the ice tea. The women poured ice tea and joined the men.

Ken tapped the table and spoke up. "Louise, there's going to be an auction here for the cattle in a few days. People are expected to come from all over, Sam said." He shifted in his chair. "Would you like to make some baked goods and sell them?"

Louise clapped. "Sylvia, will you help me bake and work with me in the sale?"

"Well." Sylvia saw Jon nod, and she answered, "Sure, I'll help. It should be fun."

The days flew by, and finally, the big day came, and people were everywhere. There were campers, hauling trucks, and tents. Jon stood staring while Ken tried to count them.

Jon said, "Between you ladies there, you've baked at least a hundred homemade pies. Louise, save me a piece of apple."

"Don't forget me. I'll have a big piece of peach." Said Ken.

Louise smiled as Sylvia shooed them away.

When the auctioneer took a break, the men wandered over to the ladies. "Pie, please."

Sylvia joined Jon and Ken at their table. Ken, in between bites, said, "I wanted to raise specialty horses for certain events. The market buying is better right now with horses than with cattle, so I decided it's the time to switch."

Jon patted Ken on the shoulder. "Ken, you're a businessman through and through."

The day was long, and had been a huge success. The men stood around talking and patting themselves on the back. The women worked together cooking the evening meal.

Sara offered to help in the kitchen, but her mom and Sylvia ran her out to address the table. She hummed as she put each place sitting down. *The fork to the left of the plate, and knife and spoon to the right. The water glass above the knife.*

Everything looked grand, and the foods smelled tempting. The dinner bell rang, and all gathered around the table. They held hands, and Jon gave the blessing. They sat down, and the chitchat began. It sounded like a swarm of bees.

The ladies cleared the table, and everything was back into its place. Sara was on pins and needles. She had overheard Ken talking with Jon earlier that today after dinner he was going to surprise her with the unveiling of the rooms. Sara was all fumbles. She clasped and unclasped her hands.

Ken motioned for everyone to sit around the parlor table and play a board game. He had selected a game, and it was Monopoly. Sara's jaw dropped. She gasped, but took a seat. Jon and Sylvia sat to her right, then Matthew, Louise, then Timmy, and his dad, Ken.

The game was underway, and they were whooping it up. Ken was trying to drive a bargain with Louise about the Boardwalk group. He laid on the charm—thick. Louise had two hotels sitting on her property and all the houses. She flagged her hand and held it out.

Ken owned the Electric and Waterworks and was holding his own.

Jon had the railroads and was doing all right.

Sylvia was the banker and tried to keep cheating out of the game.

Timmy kept buying houses while Matthew just liked rolling the dice. He usually landed in jail.

Timmy was the encourager. "Matthew, you are just visiting. I'm coming for you."

Sara forked over her last monies to her mom. She raised a hand in plea, but in the end, she had to auction off her property.

Ken raised his eyebrows almost to his hairline. With his hands in the air, he said, "That's the way it goes, Sara."

Everyone in the room laughed, her included, until the next one was caught in her mother's web. They took a break, and Louise had excused herself, along with Sylvia, to bring freshly brewed ice tea and chocolate brownies to the table.

The game was to resume when a knock came at the front door. Ken, being closer, opened it.

"Hello, everyone."

Sara yelled. There stood Jud, Karen, and the twins, Luke and Luci. She ran and jumped up and down with her best friend, while the twins twisted loose and went over to Timmy and Matthew and high–fived each other.

They stepped into the room. Ken declared Louise the winner, and the game ended. Matthew wiggled his way over to Jud, lifting his arms. "Pick me up."

Jud laughed. He rubbed Timmy's head then placed Matthew on his lap. He played "Got Your Nose" for quite a while.

Karen sat beside Sara, holding her hand. Luke and Luci squeezed in beside Timmy. Louise passed the sweets, and Sylvia got extra glasses. Jon and the men were heavy in conversation. It was getting late, and the children were yawning and rubbing their eyes. It would soon be time for bed.

Sara stood, tapping her foot. "Ken, Jon, do I get to see my office?"

Everyone laughed. They wondered how long it would take her to surrender.

The men pulled the sheets, and dust flew everywhere. Sara coughed and screamed. "Would you look at my office? There's a display front for the purses, and look, there's a bathroom! Oh, Ken. I never expected anything like this." Her hands went to her face, and the tears fell.

The ladies joined her in a circle and shared tears. Louise got a hankie.

The men beamed with pride.

The children felt right at home Timmy swung around in Sara's office chair, while Matthew tried out the bathroom. Luke and Luci started pushing Timmy.

"Whoa, whoa," said Ken.

Jon and Jud each grabbed the kids. Looking each one in the eye, Ken waved a finger. "This area is Sara's. Do not enter her door unless she invites you in. This is her official business rooms. Read the sign. It says, Sara's Adventures." Ken chuckled. "Sorry, Sara, I was having a little pun."

She giggled. "Oh, Ken, Jon. What wonderful details you both have done, and it reads, Sara's Office. Now thank you both." She hugged Jon and then kissed Ken on the cheek.

Karen clapped. "Come on, kids. Let's get ready for bed, and I'll read."

Jud walked with Karen, placing a hand on her back. She turned and touched his cheek, and he squeezed her arm. Karen continued up the stairs with the boys, and Jud stood there staring long after she was out of sight.

Ken tapped Jud on the back. He jumped. "Hey, old boy, isn't love grand?"

Jud shook his head and smiled broadly. They walked toward the kitchen, for they had serious business to discuss. They poured another cup of coffee, and talk of bank business resumed.

Jud spread out the forms to be presented at the bank. "Ken, you know Spencer is due here tomorrow for the explanations on our new procedure."

The morning came all too early.

Jud and Ken entered the bank.

"Hello, sir. How are you adjusting to the banking business?" Jud put forth his hand.

Reaching his hand forward, Ken introduced his assistant, J. J.

"I'm wanting to venture out on my own someday, Jud," J. J. said.

"Ken's structure is a great model for you to take interest in as an understudy," Jud said.

"His supervision is challenging," J. J. said. "Just kidding. No, really, I enjoy helping others, and closing a deal is my highest satisfaction."

"You dating anyone seriously, J. J.?" Ken asked.

"No. That's what got me down here in the first place. It was a total misunderstanding, I assure you. I like to socialize but not to commit. You aren't too old to understand how it is, are you?"

"Whoa." Jud and Ken smoothed over a chuckle. "J. J., someday the snake will bite, and there won't be any antidote."

Ken motioned for J. J. and Jud to move their business into the conference room. Spencer had already arrived, and appeared to be knee-deep in the company's paperwork.

Jud held his breath and stepped back when Eurlene and equal COE in banking and older sister of J. J and ex girlfriend of his walked into the space. She was carrying a cup of coffee for Spencer. He glanced her way, and the air seemed locked with flying sparks between Spencer and Eurlene.

Jud waved a hand in front of Spencer. He seemed to be in a trance. She hadn't moved either. *Well, well,* Jud thought. *This is out of the ordinary for both of them.*

Eurlene blinked, and eye emotions were shielded. "I want to thank you, Ken, for including me in this new round of legal paperwork. And, Jud, it is so nice to see you again. I traveled back with J. J. right after that horrible storm hit here."

Jud knew he needed to walk over and shake her hand and Spencer's, but his feet felt like cement. He gave her an insistent look. She was more attractive than ever. Maybe even a little more toned. Her free-spirited fiery-red curly hair was freshly styled, and it bounced. He forced his steps forward, buttoning his coat, and offered her his hand.

His eyes slid over her. She was pure sin. The royal blue fitting dress was pencil tight. She had the ability to make most men squirm, that he knew.

Finally, they made eye contact. They both briefly smiled as he let out a held breath. "Eurlene, you look awesome as always."

They shook hands, and a nod came. There wasn't the former desire left between each other any longer, only an admiration a justifiable respect.

Jud closed his eyes long enough to give thanks. It was great to feel the relief and know their individual lives had moved forward. It was a healing, and he was exonerated. The past with Eurlene before his marriage to Karen was just that—the past.

Ken shook his head, letting out a sigh while patting Jud on the back. "Moving on with business."

Spencer cleared his throat. "Let's look at these examples I brought with me."

Time poured into hours. Spencer took off his coat and rolled up his sleeves. His silk tie had been placed in his suit pocket. He was sprawled over the table with the care and perseverance of a lion.

"Ken, your client files need to be separated into two stacks. Has that been done? One should be addressed with the client on the new tax rule, and the other stack needs a new clause on inheritance regulations to be written in for the client before finalizing. Now, do you have any questions?"

J. J. stood with a box of files. "Spencer, the files in here are separated."

Through Eurlene's thick eyelash batting, she had Spencer's attention. "Is this what is needed in the state of New York also, Spencer?"

He smiled and crossed his arms, and his muscles rippled. "Great question. I will get back with you on that, all right? I may need to come to New York in case I have any questions and forms I may need to see." Spencer winked.

Putting one foot in front of the other. "Of course, Spencer."

Gathering his things, Spencer said, "Jud, it was good we had the land contract about the land case that came up in court. We could have been in worlds of trouble right now."

Everyone agreed.

With the legal items in perspective Ken felt inclined to ask, "Would you like to come to the farm for dinner and a rest?"

"No, thank you," J. J. said. "I just want to hit the bed." He turned to Eurlene. "Sis, are you staying at the rental with me tonight?"

Everyone shifted.

As she formed the words, Jud found himself holding his breath. *What would Karen think?*

Jud patted Spencer's back and shook his hand. "You coming over to Ken's?"

Spencer's briefcase clicked, and he angled his body to look directly at Eurlene. "No, not this time. I scheduled a flight out tonight." He rolled down his sleeves and slipped on his jacket. "My flight leaves in just an hour. I'll have to hurry." He squared his shoulders and thumbed his lapel. "Gentlemen, I have some unfinished business with Eurlene."

Their eyes met and held.

"Jud, Ken, now you have my answer." Eurlene shifted, and her shoes clicked. "I'm headed out likewise."

There was a click-clack of heels as the men stared after Spencer. He raised his elbow, and together, arm in arm, never losing eye contact, he and Eurlene walked out the door.

J. J. had disappeared from the room, and apparently had left. Jud nudged Ken. "Eurlene and Spencer make a smart, good-looking couple, don't you think?"

"Spencer better watch his moves with this one. His bachelorhood days are in grave danger."

Ken and Jud shook their heads, laughing.

"I'll stand at the door, ole friend, while you lock up," Jud said. "Let's get out of here and back to our loving wives."

"Hop in, Jud, and hang on," Ken said.

"Ken, don't hot-rod this time." Jud grabbed the seat. "You crazy fool."

The only sounds each other heard were that of the grinding motor and their own laughter.

17

The doorbell bellowed. It was followed by a loud continuing knock. Sara, being in her office, went and answered the door. She adjusted her skirt and smiled at the lady standing in front of her. "Hello. May I help you?"

The lady was smartly dressed in a European suit. She smoothed wisps back into her striking chignon. A child stepped from behind, who joined her. He was wearing an expensive three-piece suit. He appeared between eight and ten years old.

"Is Kenneth home?" the lady asked.

Sara squinted. "No, he isn't, but he is expected home soon. Can I help you?"

The midtwenties woman abruptly spoke. "No. Thank you. I need to speak with him. I'll wait. So do we stand outside here in the heat, or do we come in?"

Unsure of her memory, Sara added, "I'm sorry, do I know you? I recently was in an accident, and my memory is still some-what shaky."

For a moment, Sara thought she saw an empathetic look, but the woman's eyes shielded and grew dark. "No, you don't know us. We have never met, and mostly likely you haven't even heard about me—us." She stood as a stone statue. "I was looking for Mr. Jon News, Ken's father, but he didn't answer at his residence."

Jon, hearing voices, came and stood behind Sara, wanting to be supportive. "Can I help?"

Sara felt his breath on her neck. She turned and found Jon pale. His hands were in fists by his sides.

"What are you doing here?" Jon asked.

Sara blinked. His eyes were wild. "Jon, Jon!"

Sylvia heard the stern voices. She arrived at the door, paused, and then pushed past Jon to the woman. She flung her arms around this strange woman and began crying.

Sara looked past them and saw Ken's car. He had parked in the drive with Jud. She slipped from the doorway and from Jon, Sylvia, and this woman with the child, and ran to Ken. She couldn't control her trembling.

In his gentle, cooing voice, and with his eyebrows lifted, he asked, "Sara, what's wrong? What's happened?"

Sara flung her arms around him, squeezing him to feel secure. "Ken, there's a woman and a boy on our porch asking for you. Your dad came to the door and flew into a rage. He scared me. Your mother showed up at the door and all but knocked us down. She's holding this woman and crying uncontrollably."

Ken sidestepped her and went paler than his milky color. He pushed Sara into Jud's arms and took off running toward the porch and the woman.

Sara broke loose and followed after Ken.

Jud caught her and held Sara. "Wait, Sara."

She heard her husband call the woman Squirt. Ken swung the woman around.

"Put me down this instant." The woman shifted her feet and straightened her skirt. "Ken, meet your nephew."

Sara's head twirled. She pinched herself to see if she were in the twilight zone.

Ken gave the woman another whirl because he could. Her six-inch heels went flying.

The woman was mean. She pounded on Ken's back. "Put me down. Now!"

The boy was still standing like a tin solider, although his eyes were dancing and he had a faint smirk.

From the corner of Sara's eye, she saw Jon move with a tremor. Sylvia flicked her fingers, motioning him to move, and she brought the woman and boy into the house. Sara poked Jud, and they followed closely behind.

Sylvia had red-rimmed eyes but wore a beautiful smile. "Sara, come here. I want you to meet someone."

Sara's feet seemed to drag, and she offered her hand outwardly.

"Sara, meet Ken's sister, Mariah," Sylvia said. "And this is her son, Miechael."

"What?" Sara exclaimed.

"Sara?" Jud stepped forward and caught Sara on her way down.

Sara's hands flew to her head. "I'm dizzy. I think I'm going to pass out."

Jud carried Sara into her new office and placed her on a soft sofa. Sylvia and Louise came into the room, and Louise placed smelling salts under Sara's nose. She coughed and bolted upright. Ken placed an ice pack on the back of her neck and then returned to his sister's side.

Jon paced on the floor, and chatter came from everywhere. Sara needed quiet. She lay back down and saw her boys enter the room.

Karen knelt beside her, and Sara whispered, "Will you take the boys out from here?"

Sara blinked. Karen was gone, and so were her boys. She tried to sit up, slowly this time. Looking around the room, she focused and saw Jud, Ken, Jon, Sylvia, her mom, and the two strangers. *Wait, they are family.*

"Ken, how did you know this was your sister?" Sylvia asked while tapping her foot.

Sara glanced. Jud had left the room.

"Mom, let's sit and breathe." Ken walked over and took Sara's hand. "It was a long time ago, Mom. I went into your closet and found a box with pictures in it. I thumbed through them and brought the box to my room." He gave Sara's hand a squeeze. "It was my junior year in college, and I had come home for a two-week visit. If you remember in a photo, I saw a young female that looked enough like you, Mother, to be you, so I brought the photo to you and asked if it were you."

Ken flinched. "You were quick to say no, and grabbed the box of pictures, but I still had her photo. I placed it in my wallet, and that night, you and Dad were talking."

Ken walked over to his mom, and his knuckles lightly grazed her cheek. "It was late in the evening, and I needed to use the restroom. I was afraid of disturbing you and Dad, but you two were heavy in conversation. An hour or so passed, and sleep was floating in when Dad raised his voice. You said, 'Jon, you didn't have to marry me!'

"Dad cleared his throat. I heard him say, 'Sylvia, I love you. I always have, even when you became engaged to Harold.' Dad told you how it saddened his heart to see how you suffered your fiancé's death. He even mentioned the car accident."

Sylvia let out a gasp, and grew pale.

Ken went on explaining as he looked toward Sara then at his sister, Mariah. She was pointing for her son to sit down. Mariah's jaw twitched.

Jon scooted beside Sylvia and held her hand. Ken moved over to his sister. With arched brows, he reached for her hand. She jerked a little. Ken patted her hand. She slid back, and Ken began. Looking at his father, he said, "Dad, you told Mom you wanted to raise her child as your own. You betrothed your love and promise. You told her maybe she would bear a child later for you, if God willed. You also said you understood her weakness at how she had succumbed to being with him only the one time."

Nodding, he continued, "Dad, I knew my sister and I were loved, and I hoped we would get the chance to know each other, except only twice had I seen Lady and Duke Ma Mere."

Mariah squealed. "What?"

"Sis, times were hard, and Mom's family spurned Dad, for they had not accepted him," Ken explained. "He was a commoner. When they found out Mom eloped and married Dad, well, they dug until they found out a reason why Dad rushed the marriage. Dad has had a difficult time."

Ken let out a sigh. "Our parents struggled with finances, and Mother disputed with Grandma Ma Mere. Sis, they tried to buy you, but Mom would have no part of it. During the time I was born, Grandma Ma Mere pressured Mom into agreeing for your schooling abroad. Mom went to school abroad, and she wanted you to have the same opportunity also, so she agreed with her mother and father to let them send you. She needed her parents, and some peace."

Mariah stood. "Ken, I never considered you knew about me. What a loss, my brother." She heaved a sigh. "When Mom and Jon sent me abroad, I was crushed. I felt unwanted and unloved by Jon. It was there I learned I had a brother. I was both happy and sad at hearing the news."

Sylvia cried. Jon reached out to comfort her.

"At first, being away from Mom seemed unbearable," Mariah went on. "Then one day. I had visitors. It was Lady and Duke Ma Mere."

"Mariah, did they tell you who they were?" Sylvia asked.

Ken lowered his eyes. "I received a few birthday cards over the years and only two Christmas cards from the Ma Meres. They're wealthy, aren't they? Mariah, they chose you over me. They even went to see you. My sister."

Sara shook her head and began fanning herself. Was what she had just experienced and heard real? She pinched herself. She muffled yelling out. Had she ever known those people? The march of life was surely taking another turn.

Sylvia stood and raised her hands. "Let's eat something. We'll talk more about this later. Miechael, you wash up and change, then come and help me. Ken, you help your father, and, Sara, why don't you show Mariah to a room?"

Mariah hit the table. "Wait a minute."

Sylvia pulled a face of royalty, narrowing her eyes, and Mariah backed down.

Sara stared as a different aura about her mother-in-law's ways and speech was seen and heard. She was not in any mood to buck an order.

Mariah walked with Sara, and paused. She took a deep breath. "Thank you, Sara, for your kindness. Ken is a lucky man to have you as his wife."

Sara's neck turned red to her face. "Thank you, Mariah."

Sara left Mariah at the room and quickly stepped into hers. New feelings flowed through her. Sara wanted to dress up for the evening meal. She rummaged through the closet, but almost everything was lost in the crash. She moved a back hanger, and there was the outfit she had worn before Matthew was born. The anniversary yellow number.

Sara glanced into the mirror and waltzed downstairs. She felt good. Sara joined Mariah, and together, they entered the dining room.

Mariah selected a sheer blue blouse with an over-the-shoulder bow and a darker-blue pencil skirt. Her son, Miechael, seated her.

Sara wore a two-piece yellow suit with a shimmering lighter-shade blouse. Ken beamed and came behind her chair to seat her.

Sylvia waved for all the men to sit down.

Jon tapped his hand on the table. "Let's pray before we eat."

Sylvia passed the greens and spoke. "Ladies, thank you for taking the time in making this dinner special. By the looks of our men, they also appreciated the time you invested."

Sara's leg touched Ken's. She felt magnetized as he slipped a hand to her knee. She was hot and knew she was blushing. Sara sneaked a look, and Ken's smile widened.

Mariah's smile had sweetness as she flashed it on Ken. She saw he was taken in by it, but Mariah planned an attack. She passed the mashed potatoes and dug her spiked heel in his foot.

His eyebrows shot up to his hairline. Ken began sparring with his sister, and she held her own.

Mariah placed her napkin in her plate, shook her head, smiling, and asked to be excused.

Everyone followed suit. Jud had gathered Karen and the twins and walked over to Ken. He stood beside Sara and Mariah. Jud motioned for Ken.

"My friends, I want to thank you for allowing us to stay and conduct business," Jud began. "And, Sara, it's been so good to see you again." Holding his clasped hands, he said, "I'm glad you and Karen had a chance to do some girly catching up." Smiling, he went on. "As much as you two ever get caught up."

Karen punched Jud. She pouted, causing them to laugh.

Sara gave Jud a hug then Karen. "I wish you could stay longer."

"Me too, Sara," Karen said. "But the bed-and-breakfast won't run itself, and besides, I have a few purse shows to do."

Jud looked at Mariah. "Karen and I feel it's truly an honor to have met you. If you're ever in Ohio, come stay with us."

Karen joined in. "Do come, Mariah. We would love to have you."

"Ken, again thanks," Jud said. "Our flight leaves in forty-five minutes." He motioned with his hands. "Come on, gang, let's scoot."

Jon and Sylvia nodded and waved.

The children hugged each other again and again. Karen took Luci's hand, and Jud took Luke's hand and carried the luggage in the other. Over his shoulder, he spoke loudly to override the talk. "Ken, call me Friday at the office around noon."

The door closed swiftly behind them.

Ken noticed the evening had not ventured well with Mariah. It was not the manner in which she dined. She had not accepted the evening gathering nor the casual way the people appeared.

He watched as she headed toward the stairway when the doorbell dinged. She took another step and paused. Mariah looked around and saw no one was headed her way. She sighed and turned toward the door.

The bell dinged again. Mariah struggled with opening the heavy door, and the wind blew in the rain. She reached up to wipe her eyes and left her hands in midair. There stood a very tall dignified-looking man. A slick dresser. He wore a bronze three-piece suit. She gave him a quick skim. He had unusual red hair, a bit too wavy but somewhat controlled.

"Hello, lady, are you going to invite me in out of the rain?"

"And you are?" She looked intently at his electrifying blue-green eyes. Mariah straightened her shoulders and moved two steps backward. "Can I help you?"

He lifted an eyebrow and took a step inside. "Oh, you most certainly could." His smiled danced as he raised a hand, waving it at Ken. He pushed past Mariah.

"What brings you here tonight, J. J.?" Ken took his overcoat, and they headed to the kitchen. He poured J. J. and himself a cup of coffee. "Have a seat."

"Thanks for the coffee, Ken." J. J. pulled out a chair. "I'm sorry I forgot to give you this article you asked for earlier today. When I got home and showered, I remembered the article was in the pocket of my jacket. I didn't know how important it was to you, so here I am. Did Jud leave?"

"They did indeed." Ken took another sip. "Well, J. J., this was your last day under my internship. You did a fine high-quality job. I'm excited to hear about your next adventure. I hope it in a wise business movement. You have all the makings to be successful."

J. J. chuckled. "I do want to thank you for working with me as a mentor and helping me to dig out from my past. I think there's a bright future ahead." He stood and reached for his coat.

The men were near the front hall when J. J. asked, "Who's the looker?"

A hand went firmly on his shoulder. "My sister."

J.J. squared his shoulders. "Your sister?" He pitched. "Well, she didn't take after you."

Ken's eyes were almost black. He squinted. "I want you to understand she's a mother. She has a son. If there are any promiscuous thoughts on your mind, forget them."

J.J. gave off a nervous chuckle and shrugged. "I don't have any thoughts. None at all. You know I'm not looking for trouble and I'm not the marrying kind."

Mariah had posted herself on the bottom step. She was waiting to see her brother. She tapped the rail. She knew she really wanted another glance of the tall good-looking man. *That smile.*

She saw the door open, and slipped down the step, catching a heel on the throw rug. She reached for the rail, but her hand was too far away. She screeched, "Help!" She managed to place a hand on the floor hoping to break the fall.

She heard footsteps. She thought they were Ken's, but the strong arm holding her was not her brother's. He had a wicked smile, and she shivered.

"Walk much?"

She scrambled to her feet and drew back her hand.

He stepped backward out the door and flinched. Mariah slammed the door and leaned her back against it.

"Hey, sis. He's gone." Ken's eyes were dancing, and his lips were turned up. "You all right?"

Mariah pretended to straighten her already smooth skirt. "Ken, I'm sorry, but I made a terrible mistake in coming here to your home and airing my laundry." Clasping her hands, she continued, "I'm glad though we have finally met, and I think you're a grand person, but I must leave. I've already booked a flight for New York."

"Why, Mariah? I was in hope we would spend some quality time together. I really wanted to know you."

"I leave in the morning, and I have arranged for a cab to pick us up."

"Where?" Ken asked. "Do you have a place to stay or a job?"

"I'll book a hotel suite until I can make a housing purchase." She stepped away but answered Ken. "For work, I'm going to try modeling."

Ken reached for his sister and held her close. "I'm so sorry, Mariah, here did not work out for you, but traveling and not being settled, on the other hand, is not good for Miechael—or you."

Ken let out a long breath. "I have a suggestion. Please just hear me out. If you are really set on leaving, Miechael could stay with Sara and me until you find a suitable place in New York. I know the boys would love for him to stay too."

Mariah slipped from his hold. "I know you mean well." She sniffled. Thoughts reclaimed her. *The love of my life had died, and how my life had changed, and now, to part with my son.* At the moment it was too much. Tears fell.

Ken handed her his handkerchief and stood quietly, waiting for his lost sister to answer.

Mariah blew her nose. "I'll write Miechael a note to inform him of our discussion, and my decision." Walking up the steps with Ken, she paused. "Ken, all right, he can stay, but understand it's temporary. Just until I get settled."

Ken put his hand on hers. "I know leaving him behind will be hard, Mariah, but you can call and talk to your son anytime you want. I only want to help you."

She whispered, "I know, Ken."

"I'll show him around the farm and take him to a few of our county's events. He'll get to know us and how we live. It might even rub off on him."

Mariah straightened. "Remember, this is only temporary."

"Do you need any money? I have a little saved."

She turned from him, biting her lip. She willed the tears away. "No. Thank you, Ken." She flipped her head. "Grandma Ma Mere said, she would help me. I spoke with her earlier." Mariah knew she had deliberately lashed out at her brother, but she needed distance between them, for she must gain control of herself.

17

Sara caught her breath. It was already proving to be a busy morning. She was adjusting to a new youth's personality in the house. One thing was for sure: he needed different clothes. She knew Miechael's feelings were hurt when he came into the kitchen for breakfast dressed in a three-piece suit.

Timmy and Matthew were each in jeans, a T-shirt, and cowboy boots. When they looked up and saw him, they burst out laughing. Of course Timmy apologized and Matthew soon followed, but the damage had been done.

Sara served Miechael his breakfast. "Would you like to ride into town with me?"

"Yes," Miechael answered. "But why, please?"

"Well, it will give us an opportunity to get better acquainted, plus I need a few things. We can also see if the store carries your size and perhaps purchase you some different clothes to wear on the farm."

"Can we go, Mommy?"

"Good morning, boys," Sara said. "Timmy, Matthew, you're staying with your dad this time. Now come here."

The romping began. He was on the floor wrestling with his boys, and Miechael poked Sara.

He gasped. "Is he hurting them?"

Sara dried her hands. "No. Your uncle is playing."

He tilted his head. "Strange play."

"I'm done in here. Let's leave, Miechael."

Sara winked at Ken as she sat behind the wheel. "See you three in a little while. Be good."

Sara was surprised when Miechael offered her his arm. She naturally wrapped hers in his and walked into the local town's store. She watched as his hands dropped to his side and his mouth gaped open. She could only imagine by his expressions what he was thinking.

Sara strummed through the rack. "Here, Miechael, try these on. Oh, and take these."

"Where do I try them on?"

Sara pointed, and he nodded.

"It's a great fit. What do you think, Miechael?"

"Very nice. The jeans feel good."

Sara muffled a laugh.

"Aunt Sara, thank you for your and Uncle Ken's kindness." His eyes lit up. "Oh, look there's a pair of boots like Uncle Ken's."

"Do you want a pair of cowboy boots?" Sara asked.

"Ah, no. I have some scuff-around shoes."

"Miechael, I'm going to try on these. Why don't you take your purchases to the counter?"

"May I have a few leisure shirts to go with the jeans?"

"Sure."

Sara liked the way she looked in the jeans. She tucked them on her arm and headed toward the counter, but not before she picked up socks and the cowboy boots for Miechael. She thought, *He will only be little once, and he is already grown up.*

Jon was pounding again in Sara's office.

Sylvia came to see what was going on. "Oh, Jon, you really outdid yourself on this project." Patting his shoulder, she continued, "I'm so glad we came. I just wish not under the circumstances of Sara's going missing."

Facing him, she spoke, "Jon, you're a good man, and I'm proud of you. Thank you for trying to resolve the differences between you and Ken."

Jon kissed Sylvia's cheek. "We must talk."

Sylvia squeezed his hand.

"I'm so sorry for the way things happened between Mariah, Ken, and mostly you," Jon said.

"I know," Sylvia said. "I'm sorry too, but matters have a way of working out. We'll have to pray."

Jon changed the subject. "Well, Syl, you know we're scheduled today to leave. Are you ready?"

She sighed. "Almost. I need to say good-bye to Sara and to Louise, then to the grandchildren."

"I'm going to the barn to let Ken know I've finished Sara's last little extras and that we're leaving."

"I'll meet you at the car."

The screen door had a snap when it closed. Jon was always getting hit. He mumbled all the way to the barn. He looked up and flagged Ken and Sam.

"Dad, is everything all right?" Ken asked.

"It is, but it's time for your mother and me to leave," Jon said. "I've finished attaching the extra board this morning and gave it a coat of paint. That should do it."

"Dad, *thanks* is a small word to say. I want you to know I appreciated your time and for your coming here and bringing Mother. I know you care and love me. I've always known that, but I am hardheaded. I think like you."

Jon shook his head, and father and son laughed.

"You have been such a big help," Ken went on. "Sara's new addition would never have been completed in time. Dad, you made it happen."

"I know what I'm about to ask you is a lot, Ken. Will you consider bringing Sara with the boys home for a visit soon?"

Rubbing his hands, he answered, "Dad, I'll pray and think real hard about the matter. We may surprise you and come."

"We would love to have you. Things will be different. I understand my shortcomings."

Jon turned and told Sam not to work too hard, and to keep his son in line.

The men laughed.

Jon and his son embraced. It was genuine. Most issues had been settled from this visit. As they eyed each other, an appreciation and a new respect had been formed. They offered each other only new hope and faith of a possible future friendship. It lay around the next horizon and would be a new adventure.

The three boys ran to Jon. He patted Miechael's shoulder and Timmy's head. He then picked up Matthew.

"Grandpa? Grandma said to hurry before the rain begins, but I don't even see a dark cloud."

They walked over to the car, and his son was at his side. Jon addressed Timmy and let Matthew down. "I want both you boys to mind and help your mother and father. I do expect this from you."

Jon turned to Miechael. "You're an intelligent and a delightful lad. I hope you learn to relax and enjoy yourself. Your aunt and uncle are godly, loving, and caring people. Give them a chance. I love you, Miechael, boys." He embraced his son again. "I'll call when we arrive home, so you don't worry."

"Grandpa, I love you," Miechael said.

Jon embraced Miechael. "And I you, Miechael."

With a playful cuff on the arm, Jon turned from Ken and seated Sylvia in the car.

Ken squatted, looking into his mother's eyes. "You are a beautiful person, Mom. I appreciate and love you. Take care of Dad, and write me." He tapped the side door, and rose.

Sylvia handed her son a note for Sara. It read, "I would like to hold a purse show for you. Please come. Love, your mom, Sylvia." She dabbed at her eyes. Her lip quivered as she waved with a hankie in her hand.

"Miechael?"

"Sir?"

"I like your fancy boots. You look like a real cowboy. You want to help Sam and me in the barn? You'll get dirty."

He readjusted his hat as he walked toward them. "What do you want me to do, Uncle Ken?"

"Timmy, Matthew, get out from underneath the straw stack now," Ken ordered. "Your mother is calling. Go see what she wants. Hurry now."

Sam coughed, muffling a laugh.

Being assisted to a row in first class made Mariah take note.

Yes, being bred from royalty had its points, she thought, as she adjusted her pillbox hat and straightened her silk suit. She reached for a cup of tea and sadly wished it would have been a cup of the hot brewed tea Sara had mentioned her friend Karen made. After a couple of sips, she placed the cup back on the portable table. Her mind wandered to the man J. J.

He has nice thick red hair and smiling eyes.

Mariah shook her head. She needed to put thoughts of him out of her mind; besides, she reasoned, she had a son. She took out a magazine, snapped it open, and focused on what the latest fashions were to wear.

The pilot announced, "Buckle up. We're headed in for the landing."

Being in first class, they were escorted off the plane first. As Mariah passed the next section, she saw J. J. sitting in a row behind the wheel. She raised her hand to wave, but a shovey man pushed her down the aisle.

Mariah stretched, looking for J. J.'s exit from the plane. Disappointment threatened, but she forced her feet to walk toward the baggage station and retrieved her luggage. Mariah flagged a cab and took a step. She was opening the door when a man slid in front of her and entered the cab.

Her nostrils flared. She reached her hand in and grabbed the man by his suit coat. He was not getting by with terrible manners.

He looked up, locking eyes with her, and both were shocked.

"J. J.?" Mariah exclaimed. "What do you mean taking my cab?"

"Yours? Where are you headed? I'll share," he offered, speaking with his low voice and with smile lines dancing around his blue-green eyes.

"I'm booked at the new hotel on Sixth Avenue."

"It's on my way." He slid over. "Hop in."

"Well, lady, I don't have all day," the driver said. "The meter is ticking."

Mariah sat down, but there wasn't much room. She knew from his look he had the expression of the cat and canary.

"Here's the hotel. Who's paying?" the driver asked as he reached over the seat with his hand out.

Mariah rummaged for her money and found she had only her charge card with her. J. J., not wavering with his intent look, said, "I'll bail you out if you'll have dinner with me sometime soon." He brushed past her as he opened the door.

Mariah nodded as she put her arms around her stomach. It was rumbling, and not from hunger. She scooted from her seat and hurried to the coffee shop next door of the hotel. She watched him seek her, but he disappeared in the crowd.

Mariah, you coward, she thought. *Just get the money and send a courier to his place with payment of half the cab fare. Good idea, but where was he staying? Dumb, dumb.*

She poked her head out the door and shuffled into the hotel. She felt a little despondent.

"Hello, I'm Mariah News. She waited for recognition from the hotel manger. My key, please."

She looked around at the unfinished suite. She grumbled, "I need a hot very hot bubble bath." She flipped on the light and stomped to the tub. She started the water and measured the scented oil, salts, and gave an extra portion of liquid bubbles. Her robe was on the hook behind the door, with the matching gown and slippers.

Slipping into the tub, she gently squeezed the bubbles over her. She added a touch more of hot water and sank down and rested her head against the back. Miechael came to mind. She would give him a call after soaking.

Lying there, her mind strayed to the dreadful news once again of how she heard about Professor Swisfer, her beloved darling. In the beginning, it had been so wonderful to take an art class of his. Watching and knowing the love and passion he shared in each and every stroke he used to brush, forming a masterpiece.

A smile began forming when she considered the first time they met. Mariah had dropped her books, and her much-needed project papers flew everywhere. He stooped and picked up her books and papers. She sighed. It was in the hallway at the university her freshman year where they were attending, he as a teacher and she as a student.

Their hands touched, but briefly, and in that moment, it became magical. They both sensed it. She could see it in his eyes and his body language. She had an instant attraction for him, although they could not—and did not—pursue any feelings.

She felt a drip, and placed her toe to the faucet. She enjoyed his class, whether watching him speak or stroke or sashay in or out from the building. That led with her signing up for his classes over the following two years. She chuckled at the memory.

Remembering eased her pain at his loss. Being that it was her senior year, she was used to almost living at the library. One late evening, she was cramming for a test using old history dates and events' time lines. Everyone had left the library, and the keeper had asked her to make sure the door was closed and for her to listen for the old lock to click when she left.

Mariah ran more water and splashed the bubbles around her. She remembered it was a warm summer night, and walking was what most university people did. As Mariah stepped from the library to the curb, a car whizzed by. She would have been hit, except there was her knight in shining armor, the Professor, Mr. Swifter. He moved without any effort, and was quick and graceful. His large football hands and lean European body went into motion, lifting her up and out of the car's way. She stood shaking because of him, or was it the mishap with the car? She didn't know until he wrapped his arm around her and asked, "You okay?"

"No. Yes. I'm fine now." Mariah had touched his shoulder. "Thank you for my rescue."

That year, she had moved off campus to a single-dwelling row house. It was her senior year, and she was still infatuated with the professor. She had tracked him and saw there was no one special in his life. Her mind kept playing tricks on her. She imagined being next to him and wanting more.

Her grandparents had come for a visit and bought her some stylish clothes.

The end of her senior year approached, and Mariah found he was helping out at the dance. She pulled in a favor finagling her way onto the committee. They gathered and planned a senior theme. They met to decide which band to book.

She watched him when he moved. How careful he was to take extra steps away from her, or he would wait until she was seated and then would walk to the other side. Funny, was it in his touch, or the way he looked at her, saying and not saying anything? His powerful presence overwhelmed her.

Mariah straightened in the tub and added another cap of bubbles. She remembered being on the dance floor with the principal, who had two left feet. She had plastered a smile on her face until he was tapped on the shoulder by the professor and he stepped in. My, the grandeur of his steps. The waltz was beautiful, and she melted. When the dance ended, he didn't take a break, and neither did she. They danced the next dance, and she questioned if she were floating.

Most students had left. At the close, they cleaned the tables and the floor where they touched hands. He flipped off the lights, and the gym darkened.

She tilted her head back, lying in the tub, and thought it was clear as yesterday. On her tiptoes she arched and brushed his lips with hers. She had to know how he tasted. He took her arms and distanced himself, but she felt his tremor.

They walked outside. Mariah looked deep into his dark eyes, but he appeared cool and in control. She knew she was far from being composed.

They walked, distancing themselves twelve inches apart from each other to her row house. She invited him in for a cup of hot tea. Her graduation from the university had passed, and she informed him that she was no longer a student.

He studied her for a few moments then stooped and crossed her doorway. He finally said, "Tea sounds fine."

She flirted and put on some light music and lit candles. His aftershave smelled intriguing. She came behind him as he was sitting on the sofa, wrapping her arms around him, and brushed his cheek with a kiss.

He quickly stood. His eyes were sober and smoky. "Mariah, I will only give my heart once to a woman, and it's taken." He turned, she thought, to leave.

She put her hands to her heart, and she hadn't realized she was holding her breath.

"My sweet cherie, you are so young. Are you sure about me, us?"

Nodding, she brazenly spoke. "I was ready from the first time we met. Over the four years I have secretly fallen hopelessly in love with you, Professor."

He took her hands in his. "Mariah, I've searched for someone like you all my life. I had resigned never to marry. Then the day we met, I held out hope, for I knew you were the only woman for me. It's been so unbearable being near you these many years. All this time, and to still hold you afar. To push you away and trying never to dream about there being an us was punishment. You are the air I breathe."

He removed his jacket and shoved the sofa from them. He reached for her, and she glided into his arms. She unbuttoned his shirt to the third button. His chest seemed solid, and just a trace of hair was sprinkled across. Their hearts were synchronized. He lean down and blew a kiss behind her ear. She shivered.

"My darling, have you never been with a man?"

Mariah hung her head and could not answer. Her shifting and uneasiness and pink glow told on her.

A breeze crossed her face. The water had grown cold and she felt like a prune. Mariah reached for the oversized fluffy towel and pulled the stopper. She sat on a dressing bench, noticing a chip off her colored toenail. She pulled her leg up and bent to dab a touch of recolor. After admiring the effects, her mind drifted again.

He was standing so close the air felt like it stood still, waiting on his command. She stood and crossed her arms.

"Mariah, will you marry me? We can have a long courtship," he offered, with an eyebrow lifted. "Or not."

Her hands began to shake and then her whole body. She took his hands in hers. "Yes. I will marry you. It's an honor to be asked by you." She looked into his eyes. "Let us forsake a courtship. I love you, Philie. How long would we have to wait before we can have a civil ceremony?"

He had stroked his chin and held her fast. "Cherie?"

18

Mariah was cleaning and expecting Philie. Her phone rang, and it was her grandparents.

"Mariah, glad you're home. Mr. Swifter called and bluntly asked us for your hand in marriage. We've done a background check on him."

Mariah threw the dust rag and heaved a sigh.

"Are you listening?"

"Yes. To you both! I love him, Grandmother, and he loves me. We will be good for each other."

"Mariah, you have our blessing. With him being a professor and living frugally hasn't hurt. He really is quite wealthy."

"Grandmother, really!"

"Mariah, with him being older, he appears very wise. We know he adores you. Now listen. We want you to wait and have a royal wedding with all expenses paid."

Mariah gasped and stomped her foot. "We'll talk about our wedding plans at a later time." She wanted to just hang up, and she struggled for control. "Thanks, Grandmother, Grandfather for calling. Be well. Kiss, kiss. Bye."

The doorbell dinged. Mariah's heart did a flip-flop as she rushed to the door. She threw her arms around him. "Philie, we must talk. I need for you to just understand. Shush."

Mariah pleaded with Philie for over an hour.

"Will you take care of the necessary birth certificates and the certificate of Non-Impediment? The information I received said it could take up to twenty-one days to be done. It needs done at once."

She stepped away from him and took his hands. "Oh please, Philie." She assured him they would have a royal wedding later, like her grandparents wanted, but now she just wanted the satisfaction and a final chapter with a marriage to her beloved professor.

He slumped back into the wide chair.

Mariah sat on his lap and kissed him. "Please. I don't want to wait any longer to be your wife. Do you trust me?"

She stood and wrung her hands as she faced Philie, explaining her family's issues and circumstances concerning Duke and Lady Ma Mere. She took his handkerchief and blew her nose. Mariah continued about the strained relationship her grandparents had with her mother and Jon. She also told him that tension brewed between Jon and herself. It was terrible.

"I have a half brother also." She looked at him. "We've never met. So sad. I believe my grandparents have something to do with our family problems. It's probably over prestige, power, education, and money."

Philie took her hands. "Mariah, let's be sensible about us and think. We can work out all these frictional matters completely out one by one. We have time."

Mariah bit her bottom lip. "Philie, I've waited long enough for my professor. Haven't you waited also?" She touched his arm. "Together as one, we could face anything. Please, Philie?"

Time seemed to stand still as she waited for his answer.

He paced back and forth, holding his arms across his chest. She flopped and thought about the tragedy of his parents' death and the unsolved train wreck and how his parents were so young. She glanced and silently pleaded with him and waited.

She recalled how Philie had graduated from high school and the university by the tender age of twenty-one. He was well respected and had carried himself well as a student, so when he applied for a position at the university, even at his young age, he was quickly accepted.

Philie stopped in front of Mariah and pulled her up. Her heart was beating so loudly she thought, *He must hear.* He held her at arm's length.

"All right, my love, you I can not resist." He let out a long breath. "We'll marry as soon as the paperwork clears. There will be no family invited, only us. You can call your mother or write her to let her know our plans. One must always strive to keep contact even in the hardest of times."

She entwined her hands in his hair, throwing back her head. "I'm so happy. All I need is you."

After a lingering kiss, he smiled. "We'll face your family together and have another ceremony at their request, darling." He picked her up and swung her around.

Life, at the moment, was good.

Mariah's eyes were flecked with amber warmth, and she blushed. The next day, stepping on clouds, she purchased sheer nightwear, under items, and an ivory two-piece suit. She found a matching hat with a detail plume, gloves, and gold sling-back shoes, with a matching beaded clutch purse for their civil ceremony.

She didn't see much of her professor over the next three weeks, only a few phone calls and an occasional meeting. Their day finally came. She walked with bright steps as she entered the ceremony area. She glanced around and saw her Greek man. He was breathtaking. Tall, lean, stern structured, muscular, and very nicely dressed in a new dark three-piece suit. He was holding flowers—daisies.

As the light glazed his eyes, darkness and fieriness appeared. She felt drawn to their deep pool. His black hair touched his collar but was slicked back with cream or oil, and a stubborn wave promised to give way.

He held out his hand, and the unfathomable smile assured Mariah of his sincere intent. They joined hands, and she was held by his heartfelt pledge of love. The look he shared as he slipped on the exquisite mother of pearl ring of his late mother's onto Mariah's finger, saying, "With this ring I thee wed" caused a shiver, and another threatening round of joyful tears to flow from her.

Mariah trembled as she thought how their passion was electrified as he was authorized to kiss his bride. She hadn't hurried his slow approach. His lips were soft, and he was wholly and undeniably male. They stopped to eat, but not a bite was taken to their lips. They moved through the streets arm in arm, as if there was no tomorrow. Lingering only for a kiss or two, they passed fountains and tossed in coins. They laughed and stopped for more kisses. This was the beginning of the rest of their lives.

They stayed at a flat in town belonging to a friend of his who was away on a holiday in the States. The flat was nothing exceptional, but what mattered was him being there with her. For now, the place was theirs. There weren't any phones, or family, and no troubles—only their melted time together of never-ending love. It was a total ecstasy.

After three all-too-short days of bliss, they journeyed to her row house for her to start packing. She would be moving in with him at the housing supplied by the university for senior professors until he transferred to New York. He had given her a kiss then pulled her deeper into his arms and swore of his undying love to her. His kiss had intensified, and she surrendered. He pinched her bottom, and his lips twitched with a wicked smile.

"Be back soon, my love."

The door closed as he left to sign papers waiting for him at the university for their living arrangements.

She recalled hours had passed. She had paced the small area, being concerned and waiting for her professor. She dressed in warmer clothes and reached for a wrap. There was a knock at the door. She wondered it must be Philie. Silly her. She had forgotten to give him a key.

She flew to the door and flung it widely open. Her jaw dropped. It wasn't him but his friend who was back from the

States. Her stomach plunged on its own roller coaster, looking at his face. "How may I help you?"

"May I come in?" There was a chill in the air.

As Charles, his friend, stepped in the foyer, he said, "Would you mind brewing us some hot tea? Make it strong, please."

She nodded and went into the kitchenette. He followed and leaned on the counter. "Mariah, what I need to say is very painful, and it's a shame."

Mariah touched Charles's arm. "What is it?"

The teakettle whistled. She poured them both a tea. She slipped his over the counter. He took a sip. She added a lump of sugar and stirred.

"Come sit." He cleared his throat. "I want you to know Philie was the happiest I've ever seen him when he stopped in at the university. He was going on and on about your beauty, and he was right. He spoke of the wedding and how blessed he was to have you as his wife. He even joked a little about hoping you got pregnant soon. He wanted a girl to model the likeness of you."

Mariah blushed and scooted closer to the edge. She saw in his eyes hurt and an uncomfortable seriousness. "Is there something you haven't said?"

He came around the counter and knelt, placing her hands in his. "We need to depart to the hospital."

She shivered and clutched her wrap closer. She felt her heart pounding, trying to burst from her chest.

"Mariah."

She glanced at her ring and began twisting it. Quickly, she whispered, "Help."

"I'm so sorry. The hospital called the university, and I took the call. Come, we must hurry. It's Philie."

Mariah reached for her purse. The hospital was only four blocks away, and she ran. Getting to him was her only reason and desire. She didn't remember if there was any traffic or if the lights were green or red. She felt stinging tears. *Hang on, darling, I'm coming. Please help!*

Charles caught up with her. They entered the sterile hospital and its smells.

"Hello, Ms. News?"

"Yes, but it's Mrs. Swisfer."

The tall marble-like woman turned, and over her shoulder, she spoke. "Come this way."

Mariah and Charles were placed in a little side room. *Was it a broom closet? Oh, the smell—disinfectant.*

The shuffling of in-tune steps caught her attention. A man dressed in doctor's scrubs appeared. "Ma'am." His took a step closer. "Ms. News, we're sorry for your loss."

"It's Mrs. Swisfer. What did you say?"

The doctor continued, "We tried everything we could to save him, but he was too far gone."

Almost whispering, she asked, "How did this happen?"

Charles took her shaking hand.

She moved it away and stood. Biting her lip, she said, "Well?"

The doctor sounded like he was giving a weather report. "There was an impact of two cars. The authorities are looking into it. Ms. News, his last words were 'Till death do us part, my lovely cherie.' Then he expired."

Mariah couldn't breathe. Her lungs ached, and she felt dispirited. "I need to see him." She twisted her wedding ring.

They walked the gray corridor in all its dreary sterility. She heard her steps, or was it her heart breaking? Charles gave her time alone in Philie's room.

She mustered her courage. Mariah took his now-pale hand, which once was tan, and cried. The tears spilled until her rims were swollen and red. She felt a tap on her shoulder, and glanced up.

A rigid-looking nurse stood tapping her foot. "Madam, you need to leave. I now need to make arrangements. We have already spoken with Charles, and he assured the university had covered him with insurance should there be a death. He left a will for his body to be used for research. Time is of the essence." The nurse touched Mariah's shoulder. "Again, sorry for your loss," she added as she marched Mariah through the door.

Mariah felt her knees buckle. Once again, she was in that small disinfectant-smelling room. She was handed a plastic glass half-filled with orange juice.

Charles placed his hand on her arm. "I'm so sorry, Mariah, but please excuse me. I need to help the doctors attend to business, for they have papers for me to sign. Go home. Call and be with your mother, or Grandma Ma Mere. Mariah, leave! He's gone. I'll see to it you receive a remaining check from his insurance." He adjusted his tie and wheeled out from the room.

She was floundering, but rose and somehow walked to the row house and began to unpack. She made a tea and cried some more. What was she to do? She felt so alone. She looked at his picture and then at a snapshot of them taken on their wedding day. She twisted her ring.

"It's over."

She sunk into the sofa and cried herself asleep.

The next morning, it rained. Mariah pulled the covers over her head. She wanted to die, but she was very much alive. Days passed, and Mariah heard from no one. It was like living a nightmare. She needed to call someone, but whom? She wallowed in self-pity. Was God even listening? *See me. I'm hurting.*

Days had turned into weeks and months. Mariah did not feel well, and there had been definitely a weight loss. Her clothes became baggy, where they once fit snugly. She ate little, for food smelled awful. Her stomach began having twitches.

Mariah was shaky, and decided hunger had set in when she awoke. She didn't know why, but a pot roast came to mind and sounded good. The local store was within walking distance. On her way home, the sun peered brightly. Had it been shining? It seemed it was beckoning her to breathe with each step she took. Even though her heart ached, Mariah decided to begin making a day's plan for her future.

She contacted a doctor to see what added vitamins she needed for her diet but was surprised to find out her need would be for prenatal care.

She contacted her grandma Ma Mere and explained her disobedience of her and Philie's marriage. She apologized for disobeying but couldn't help expressing how grateful she was for the time they had had. Mariah choked as she spoke of the baby and assured Grandma Ma Mere she was carrying it to full term. She removed any notions about giving the baby up for adoption. They promised Mariah a fund would be wired in a savings account for the baby's expenses. They explained she needed to consider future plans and think even now on the education of her child.

She knew they would definitely be in her life for support and instruction, but it was of no comfort.

"Stand strong, Mariah, and don't crash. After all, you are made of royalty. Finish your master's degree, and find your backbone breeding."

The words from her grandparents stung but carried her through as well as their money. She gave birth to a wonderful eight-pound baby boy, Miechael, and he was big but healthy. Other than the wave in his hair and apparent build, he favored his mother. His sweetness and patience was bred into him from his father, and that smile.

His great-grandparents were actively involved placing Miechael in boarding schools. They paid for everything. Her son was being raised as she had. Over the years, Mariah had missed her mother, Sylvia. Mariah had sent her one letter explaining she was returning to the States on a holiday, and briefly mentioned her son.

Mariah now shuddered at how that visit went at her brother's. She committed to memory how Ken had accepted both her and her son. She laughed. Then there was precious Sara. An instant warm liking came, and she was never judgmental. Sara stood by her husband and was determine to be helpful. She was a great example being a woman of God who appeared sincere about wanting a relationship with her.

Mariah fluffed her hair and gloomily reached for the phone and dialed the lobby, asking for a night snack of hot tea and toast to be sent to her room. She opened her suitcase to retrieve her nightclothes, and there she spotted an envelope addressed to her. Mariah let out a moan. Could she possibly handle any more? She slipped into her nightwear and placed on a robe.

She held the envelope and quickly opened it.

Dear Mariah,

I overheard you and Ken speak of your leaving. I'm so sorry we didn't get more time in getting to know each other better. I've always wanted a sister, and now, I have one. The closest to a sister before now is my best friend, and you met Karen. She's the best, but you and I could have a real bonding relationship also, if you would just give us half a chance and try.

I know you're on an adventure, and I have had my share. Only you can settle the battle raging inside yourself. Remember, you are never alone. Mariah, when I was lost from the plane crash and didn't remember anyone I was quoted this verse, Romans chapter 8, verse 39. It reads, "Nor height, nor depth, nor any other creature, shall be able to separate us for the love of God, which is in Christ Jesus our Lord."

There is another verse that I cling to, and it still helps me. It is found in 1 Peter, chapter 5. verse 7: "Casting all your care upon him; for He careth for you."

Mariah, I'm here for you. Please call or write me. I hope you enjoy the trendy purse that I made and also packed in your suitcase.

Your son is in good hands. He'll be well taken care of until you return. We love him so. Miechael is a lot like you! Be sure and keep in touch.

Your newly found sister in Him, and with love,

Sara

Mariah felt drained from the travel and her reflections from the past. She was now faced with present and long-ago facts, and they were still haunting her.

The doorbell dinged. Mariah looked forward to drinking the tea. She paid the bellhop and tipped him before closing the door. She set the toast down and smelled the tea. She brought the cup to her lips and took a sip. She began to settle after eating most of the toast and half the tea. Mariah picked up her pen and wrote, "I need a job. Modeling? More money. I'll call Grandma Ma Mere. Call a realtor. Hmm. Why not a penthouse suite?"

The phone rang. She jolted and answered the phone. She hoped Miechael was all right. "Ken?"

"Hello, Mariah." The voice was intriguing. "No, it's not Ken. This is J. J."

"Who?"

"It's J. J. I was wondering…"

Mariah dropped the phone. Her heart was beating too quickly. Panic rushed in, and then bitterness of an uninvited stranger's intrusion set in. She heard him calling her name as she slammed down the phone. Mariah's mood needed to be adjusted. She took the last few sips of tea and crunched on her cold toast.

Her mind roamed. *J. J. was nervy, bold, and attractive—no, no, not attractive. He was handsome and a head taller than I. His assured ways and strutting self-confidence came through. He had welcoming blue-green eyes that crinkled when he smiled. J. J. took my breath away.*

She made a fist and said, "Creep. He's nosey." Her mind couldn't help thinking J. J. was a tempting and a desirable man. She admitted to herself she had feelings, for her stomach had twanged with pangs, plus her heart skipped a beat from the sound of his voice. What was wrong with her?

She slammed the dresser drawer. She definitely didn't need anyone extra in her life, and with that settled, Mariah picked up the phone and called management to ward off J. J.'s calls. Should he try again? Mariah then had the night manger place her call over to a night switchboard operator.

Mariah shifted. She was through with any thoughts about spirited, self-assured J. J.

"This is the operator. May I help you?"

"Please connect me to a Mr. Kenneth News of Mississippi."

"It's ringing."

"Thank you."

Ken picked up the phone.

"Hello, Ken. I've arrived here safely, and this is my number." She heard paper rattling. "How is my son?"

"Mariah, please come back to the farm and let's work through our problems," Ken said. "Sara and I would love that so much."

There was silence, and she didn't answer, so Ken continued. "Miechael is well and is no problem. You have done a great job raising him."

"Thanks for the offer about coming, Ken, but I need time to ponder and work through my many issues, beginning with employment, unless I go live with Duke and Lady Ma Mere," Mariah said. "Take care, and I'll be in touch. Tell Sara thanks for the letter. I'll write." She let out a sigh. "Ken you did well when you married Sara. I care for her too. Her kindness is real, and it shows." She cleared her throat. "Kiss, kiss, Ken. Ciao."

"Mariah, I love you." Ken held the phone, listening to the dial tone after she was gone.

19

Sara thanked her mother, for the picnic was awesome. She knew her mother always brought out family values and true wholesome fun. The boys had enjoyed their running, rolling, and jumping on the ground. Funny how Ken had joined right in there with the boys. Their laughing sound was rewarding.

It was really good seeing Timmy, Matthew, and their cousin Miechael talking, playing, and getting along so well. Matthew yawned, and he just couldn't keep his eyes open any longer. He ventured over to Louise and curled up on the blanket with his grandmother while she read.

Ken whimsically flirted and was attentive with Sara. He stooped and picked a bunch of wildflowers and handed them to Sara. She noticed his Stetson shaded his eyes and kept her from interpretation. Ken stood with his ebony hair slicked back. He was wearing a wavy ponytail. He had placed a wheat blade between his lips, and a slight dimple was forming. He offered his hand to her, and she obliged.

She thought, *What a blessing it is to have a second chance at life.*

Sara paused, taking a moment to look upward toward the heavens and acknowledge His grace and power.

Ken bent forward, giving her a kiss. She wasn't timid pulling back, but an undying urge began burning within her soul. She stretched, placing her hands at the side of his hair, whispering, "I love you, cowboy."

He let out a long sigh. "Tonight, after your purse show, promise you'll meet up with me at the tire swing."

She felt heat rise from her neck while she stared at his full lips and verily whispered, "Yes. I'll be there."

Ken's smile continued to deepen, showing a full dimple, and he swatted her on the bottom. He distanced himself, and his mood seemed to shift. "I have the end-of-the-month paper reports due." He shifted, turned, and walked toward the truck. Over his shoulder, he winked while tipping his hat. "See you later, Mrs. News."

Sara stood shivering. She pulled her thoughts together. As she dressed for her show, Sara wished for the first time she could stay home. She knew the drive would refresh her mood and her professionalism would shine through. She thoroughly enjoyed the interaction of people from her purse shows, and she had felt comfortable leaving the boys with her mother.

Although the boys thought they were watching Louise.

The hostess's evening party was a wonderful success. The amount of sales and bookings were tremendous. Sara had given her usual spiel about owning one's business, and Terri Reshaw a stay at home wife was hooked. Sara was amazed at the smoothness and quickness of the paperwork completeness of assigning the show over to her new recruit. Sara explained to Terri that she would make clear 25 percent of the sales. After leaving Terri with a copy of the signed business agreement and a few purses to add to her beginning, Sara hugged Terri and scurried to the car.

Sara was happy and relieved there wasn't much to reload into the car. As she focused on the drive home, her mind left the thoughts of the new recruit to dwell on her date meeting up with her serious but desirable cowboy.

As she stepped into the house, Louise reached for Sara's briefcase and said, "There's fresh cookies and a pot of hot brewed tea. Would you like me to bring you in some refreshments?"

"Mom, I sure would appreciate our having sometime together." Sara glanced at the clock, and saw she still had a little time before seeing Ken.

Louise sat with Sara, pouring herself a cup of tea while she dunked cookies. "Sara, Jud called while you were out. It's about the house." She smiled, but it was not reflected in her eyes. "The home place sold and brought in two thousand dollars over the asking price."

Sara's eyes opened wider. "Mom, how wonderful! And it didn't take Mr. Drum very long at all to sell the house."

Louise clasped her hands after dabbing at her eyes. "Jud continued saying Kate had hired an auctioneer for the furniture and whatnots in the house that was left behind, and a young couple amongst others did most of the bidding. They wanted the furnishings to stay at the house."

She sighed. "He said Kate received eighteen hundred dollars clear after all fees were paid. Then Jud shouted that the young couple also bought the house. He mentioned the young couple were expecting their first child and just fell in love with the house and the yard. When they saw others bidding so closely, they raised their number and bid above the asking price for the house, and it anchored the deal."

Louise rose and added hot tea to her cup. "I hope they'll be happy there as I certainly was in raising my family."

Sara reached for her mother's hand. "Thanks, Mother, for sharing this news, but are you really all right with the homestead being sold and with your move?"

Louise dabbed at her eyes. "Yes, I couldn't be happier." She shifted, straightening her shoulders. "Oh, Jud is sending both certified checks next week to Ken. One for the house and the other for its furnishings. Ken, at that time, will advise me on how to invest the money."

Sara moved closer and hugged her mother. She had mixed emotions herself but shared in her mother's happiness. She sighed, thinking how she missed her father.

They heard Ken come inside. Louise ushered him into the kitchen, for she had baked a batch of chocolate chip cookies still cooling. At the touch, they were warm, and the aroma was delightful.

Louise raised her trembling hand, holding her teacup, and saluted. "Here's to celebration of the sold house." She looked at Ken and then at Sara. "We're now family."

Ken kissed her on the cheek and said, "Hear, hear. Mom Louise, are you happy? If you are, I am too."

Small talk continued between the three adults. Sara filled Ken and her mother in about her new recruit.

Louise turned to Sara. "My, this business of yours has really grown."

Sara nodded. "But, Mom, sometimes doing shows gets old. It's not fun like it once was— before the accident." She bit her lip as to not cry.

Louise surprisingly asked, "Do you or Ken have any plans pressing tomorrow?"

Sara glanced Ken's way. He hunched his shoulders and shook his head.

"No, not really," Ken answered. "Why, Louise?"

Louise patted her apron then shook her index finger. "Sara, you'll need to fix a dinner for your man. Sam asked me to attend a movie with him. Or we could make it a family affair?" Louise's coloring showed a shade of darkened pink.

Sara's eyes widened as she stuttered. "Mother, you and Sam?"

Louise, still blushing, flapped her apron and stuttered her words. "Ken, Sara, it isn't anything. We are just friends!"

Ken tried to cover his smile. "You two go on ahead. I'm going to help Sara with her data entry from her show. It's a new system, and a little tricky." His voice trailed off. "We'll let the boys sleep in and play some board games later."

Ken observed Sara with dancing eyes, and she saw amusement lift at his mouth. Ken replaced his hat. "Thanks for the cookies." He began munching again as he headed toward the barn.

Ken caught sight of Sam murmuring. Ken flagged him. "Sam, wait up." Ken smiled as he helped Sam add some straw into the new horse's stall.

Ken, relaxed, mentioned, "Hey, Sam, Louise mentioned you two are taking in a movie tomorrow?"

Sam placed his pitchfork in the straw. "I didn't think I needed to ask permission, Ken."

"Ole Sam, don't get so huffy. I think it will be nice for both of you." Ken tossed a few more pitched before adding, "Her house has sold, and Louise doesn't have any ties back in Ohio now."

Sam began to whistle, and Ken walked to the radio and turned the switch lower. "Night, Sam."

"Sorry, boss," Sam said. "I'm just edgy, for I do feel an attraction toward Miss Louise."

Ken muffled a chuckle and tilted his hat. "Want me to turn the lights off?"

"Ken, hit the switch. I've got a flashlight."

Ken strolled outside, taking in a deep breath. He kicked at a stone. He had his hands in his pockets and was headed toward the swing.

"Hey, cowboy, remember me?"

He was caught by surprise. "Darlin', have I told you lately I love you?" He placed an arm around Sara, and he was smiling wickedly.

"Did you confront Sam about Mother?"

"I did, and he was a bit touchy. It took him awhile to realize I was pulling his goat."

The moonlight was streaming across Ken's face, and his features, although strong, were relaxed.

"Enough about him, Sara. How about me?"

Ken's knuckles lightly grazed her cheek, and she found he still had such a magical effect on her. Her stomach rumbled. He reached for her hand, and heat exploded.

"Dance with me, darling."

She wondered as they danced if wasn't the last time they danced a tango at Claudia's. His hand lowered, bringing her closer. He slowed his steps. "Sara," he whispered as they twirled, "may I pleasure you tonight?"

She went limp. His nearness was breathtaking.

Sara was now putty. "Oh, Ken."

He swished her up in his arms, his beautiful ebony eyes never leaving hers. He pushed open the back door, only pausing to readjust her. They reached the top stairs, and he switched on the light. Sara saw them flicker and then go off. She blushed but entwined her fingers at his nape. How they made it inside and to their bedroom, she couldn't remember. They were kissing, and her breathing became rushed. He slowed his paced, wanting her to enjoy a night worth remembering.

The air had a chilled, and he was reluctant in letting her loose, but Ken wanted to build a fire to remove the night's dampness for their added comfort. The logs soon caught fire and began crackling.

"Ken, I'll be right out," Sara said.

He sought for her hand. "You need any help?"

Sara shyly smiled and closed the door. She slipped into the shower and hurried. She was all thumbs drying off and was shakingly nervous in picking out her nightwear. Sara applied a small amount of makeup and pinched her cheeks. She tied a ribbon, which matched her gown, in her hair. Sara liked what she saw. She stepped onto the bedroom in her bare feet where she felt the warmth and noticed the romantic fire.

Ken had disappeared, and there lay a trail of his clothes leading to the shower. She tried settling the flip-flops in her stomach when he entered the room in his PJs and his shirt was partly unbuttoned. His damp tousled hair waved around his shoulders, capturing her heart once again. Sara placed a hand across her heart, for she never tired from seeing his manliness.

He moved closer, edging his way near the bed. "Can you believe Old Sam?"

Sara shook her head and touched his chest. "What about my mother? Who would have figured?"

"Darlin." She felt his warm breath.

Shyly and falteringly, she whispered, "Cowboy?"

Ken nudged Sara. "What were they thinking?"

The boys hadn't slept in, and neither could they. Ken, being helpful, made breakfast and afterward engaged in horseplay with Timmy and Matthew.

"Daddy, are you going to kiss Mommy?"

Ken took a towel, made a snapping sound, and whispered. "Let's make it a good one, Sara. We don't want to let the boys down, do we?"

Sara grinned. "No." She stood on her tiptoes. Ken slipped his hat off and held it in front of them, covering both their faces.

Matthew peeked from beneath. "He sure is kissing Mom!"

Ken looked over the hat and saw Miechael trying to muffle a laugh. "Okay, boys, shoo. Outside now."

Sara, hearing the door spring close behind them, reached and began folding clothes. Snap, fold, fold. Snap, fold, fold. She was jarred from her mind-set as a loud noise and shuffling commotion came in from outside. She knew the boys were supposed to be in the barn with Ken, and looking at the clock, she knew it was not time for Sam and her mother to be back.

Sara scurried to the kitchen window and peeked out. Oh my, there stood Claudia.

"Hey in there," Claudia called out. "Anybody home?"

Sara gazed, wide-eyed. She was speechless. Claudia had one foot on the old Ford, pickup truck's running board, and hitched to the truck was a horse trailer. What a sight. Claudia had on faded torn bibs, with a red bandana tied around her neck and a big stained hat sitting on her tied-back hair. The horn blew.

Sara quickly ran to meet her and flung her arms around Claudia. "My goodness, I'm so glad to see you! I thought you couldn't come until early spring. How did you manage to get away, Claudia?"

Sara drew back and watched. Claudia had that sideways smile. She slapped the dust from her bibs, and taking the handkerchief from her neck, she wiped at her clammy brow. "Sara, may I have a drink of water? I'm parched. My tongue's hanging out, and it feels like a ball of cotton." As if one would not understand, Claudia put her tongue out, going, "Ah. Then we'll chew the jaw."

Ken and Sam came out from the barn. Claudia astounded everyone when she picked Ken up like she was shoveling coal. Ken took Sam's shoulder as he was let down.

"Ken." Claudia flicked the bill on her stained hat.

"I won again this year at the Kentucky Derby so."

Claudia nodded in Sam's direction. "Hey, unlock the trailer here. I've brought Ken a fine stallion from ideal stock."

"What? How did I get blessed?" Ken's eyes were twinkling.

"I liked what I saw in the pictures Sara sent of the horse you bought, Ken. Well, boys, what ya still standing there for?" Claudia turned, grinning and took Sara's arm. "Here's a basket of jams I put up myself, baby girl."

Sara took the basket and peeked through the jams. "Thanks, Clo."

Claudia sat her glass down on the counter. "Thanks. Can't beat H2O." She sighed. "I best get along to the barn and see what they're doing while you're fixing lunch."

Miechael, Timmy, and Matthew came and stopped dead in front of Claudia.

"Hi, boys," Claudia greeted.

Miechael and Timmy stared. Matthew stepped forward and spoke. "Why are you not wearing a dress?"

Sara heard through the window, and gasped. Claudia threw her head back, laughing, and she placed her arms around them, herding them back to the barn. She looked over her shoulder and saw Sara's beet-red face and open mouth, and winked. "Boys, have you never seen a cowgirl?" She was still laughing.

Sara had plenty of questions, but they would have to wait until dinner. Sara worked and rolled out the noodles to let them dry, and had motioned Sam to bring in a chicken. She baked a pie and made a garden salad and had the ice tea brewing.

She slipped from the kitchen and put fresh sheets on the bed in the spare room for Claudia. Just the thought of her brought a smile. *You got to love her.* Sara shook her head. A hullabaloo was happening in the kitchen.

Sara came and let out a huff. "Timmy, what's all this mud doing in the house?"

Timmy looked pleadingly to her. "Claudia sat me in the watering trough."

Sara burst out laughing. "Why would she ever do a thing like that?"

"Mom, I jumped on her back and said, 'Ride 'em, cowboy.'"

"What? God Almighty, why?"

"We were playing—Miechael, Matthew, and I. It started out as Leapfrog. Then—"

"Mister, you get out there and apologize to Miss Claudia," Sara cut in.

"Ah, Mom," Timmy whined.

She pointed, shaking her finger. "Out the door. March." She watched him—wet, dirty, and all—walk like a tin solider in battle over to Claudia. What a sight.

Sara searched out the mop and chuckled all the while she cleaned.

Ken called out to Sara, "Come out and feast your eyes on the stallion Claudia brought."

Sara placed the mop on the back porch. "My, he's breathtaking. He looks like a horse straight from a fairy tale. Look how tall, proud, and extensive he appears. He's beautiful, so pure white. Look at his mane, and isn't his tail long?"

Sara noticed the men and Claudia had already assigned the stallion to a stall. It had been bedded with straw, and the oats were poured into a feeding bag. Sara saw Sam had filled the tin bucket with fresh water for the luscious creature to enjoy.

Claudia broke the admiring silence by bellowing out, "Ken, here's his papers. Now in return, I want the first foal from him. Agreed?"

Ken nodded. "Agreed."

"Put it there, pardner." Claudia spit into her hand and offered it to Ken.

His eyes widened, and his eyebrows rose.

Sam quietly said, "Ken, spit into your hand and shake."

Ken looked from Sam back to Claudia, and with uncertainty, he spit in his hand and shook hers.

"Now that's that," Claudia said. "It is settled. Let's move into the house and sit a spell."

"After you, Claudia."

The children were still spellbound by Claudia's speech and manners, so they followed her around like a puppy. She spun tales of how the West was won, only she somehow interjected she could have been part of that move.

Softly, Sara spoke, "Let's everyone wash up, then we'll chit-chat more at the table before we eat." She wiped her hands, and heard a light knock at the front door. She checked the door, and the postman rang, calling out, "Mailman, mailman."

"Hi," Sara said. "What did you bring us today?"

"Mrs. News, there's a letter here for you to sign."

"Me?"

"Yes. Sign here."

Sara scribbled her name and squinted to see who had sent a letter. "Oh. It was from Mariah." She silently prayed as she held the letter close to her chest.

Ken entered the room first. "Sara, what are you holding?"

Before she could answer, everyone else had gathered around, waiting to hear from Claudia. Sara motioned for Ken to sit. She placed the letter in her apron pocket and gave it a little pat. She placed a hand on Ken's shoulder, joining him. Her mother was back with Sam, and she instructed the children to sit on the floor, and she took a chair near Sam. Miechael stood, but only for a second. All eyes were on Claudia, like she was their dinner at Thanksgiving.

Sara listened spellbound as Claudia talked about her bunk hand and how he arrived shortly at her place after Sara had left and come home with Ken.

"Don't it beat all." Claudia chuckled and slapped her knee. "Omar came back to the ranch driving a covered wagon with a woman. It was his wife. She was a mail-ordered bride he had sent for. I wanted them to have some time together and get settled in, so here I am." She tipped her head back, laughing again.

Then Claudia became very somber. "I will be leaving here in the morning, though. I have a day's journey yonder to meet up with an old horse trader." She thumbed her bibs, rocking on her boots. "He says he's got a horse I'd be interested in. I have to go see. It's the dealing that scares me. I don't want to be taken." Again she thumbed her bibs and went for a coffee.

They continued talking and exchanged old tales for several hours. Louise motioned for Sara, and she excused herself. The chicken was finally done.

20

Claudia came stomping into the kitchen, putting her boot on the chair rung. "Need any help?"

Sara, in a cheery voice, asked, "Would you like to pour and serve the freshly brewed ice tea and steaming coffee?"

"Let me at it." Claudia removed her foot, scooting the chair in. It made a screeching noise.

Sara and Louise both instantly covered their ears.

"Sorry," Claudia said.

Sara braved a smiled and went back to mashing potatoes, and left Louise making yellow gravy. Sara glanced at Claudia's way. "Say, Claudia, tell me, what do you hear from Jack?"

The room went silent. Sara turned, and so did Louise, adjusting her body to see her. "Claudia?"

Claudia was a bright red.

"What is it, Clo?" Sara asked.

"I already told you," she said in an unusual tone, "He asked me to come to Ohio. Jack wants us to court."

"Now, Claudia, you have met Karen, and you know about her bed-and-breakfast place, so what's the holdup?"

Claudia shifted each foot. One could hardly hear her say, "Sara, I'm scared. Me and him have feelings, but…" She shook her head. "What if it doesn't work out? I can't bear being alone again."

Sara reached out for Claudia and took her ice-cold hands. "Claudia, we need to pray for His direction."

They both went down on bended knees and closed their eyes, making no sound. The time seemed to stand still, for not a movement was made by anyone. Sara arose and brushed her apron and gave her mother a nod.

Being that it was late in the day, Louise announced, "If there are any leftovers, they will be revamped and served for supper." She chuckled. "And of course, there will be a baked desert." She looked around as she folded her hands, waiting for the food to be passed.

Everyone was stuffed. The men were patting their stomachs, and so was Claudia. They raved about the food. Sam stood first, excusing himself, and slipped out and mentioned he was tending to the animals. He held a clipboard and appeared to be making a list of things needed from the local feed store for either him or Ken to pick up.

Sara watched as her mother, Louise, excused herself from the room and slipped off her apron. She slicked a wisp of hair behind her ears and said, "I'll be right in. I'm going to look at the new horse. I understand he's magnificent."

Sara glanced at Ken, but only a slight smile appeared.

"Anyone for checkers?" he announced.

Claudia straddled a chair and raised a hand. "Ready to lose, buckaroo?"

"Bring it on." Ken had won several championships at checkers, so he was grinning like a Cheshire cat. Sara watched as Claudia sat across her opponent with narrowed eyes.

Miechael was glued to his seat, observing the moves of the players. The skipping across the board made his eyes widen. Timmy went to the shelf and got a book. Matthew reached his hands up to sit on his mother's lap. The game was almost over when Matthew squealed, "I want to play, Mommy."

Claudia plinked a spoon, and it flipped into her glass. "What-a you gotta say now, Ken?" Before he could answer, she screamed,

"Checkmate!" Claudia shifted. She gathered the checkers and toyed with the black ones. She turned to Matthew, and leaning in, she asked, "Would you like to play the champion?"

Ken was still shaking his head at his loss. Matthew shyly nodded and slid on the bench and placed his knees under him. "Red, please."

Louise came in, flushed and fanning herself. She joined in around the table, calming her breathing.

Claudia made the first move. Matthew quickly slipped his red checker into place and smiled. "Got ya."

He quickly puckered. Timmy came and placed a hand of encouragement on his shoulder as he scowled at the woman sitting across his brother. Claudia saw Matthew's deep disappointment. She began making wrong moves here and there so he could claim her checkers. "Would you look at that?" Smacking her knee, she stated, "I can't believe I just lost." Claudia thumbed her bibs. "Matthew, you must have really been watching your father while we were playing."

In his small shrill voice, he said, "Mom, did you see? I won!"

Sara nodded, giving him a big hug and a smile. The look on Matthew's face was priceless.

Louise tapped Miechael on the shoulder. "It's your turn to play your uncle Ken in a game."

Ken motioned for Miechael to take the black checkers, and he took his seat opposite. "Your move."

Louise glanced Sara's way. She mouthed, "I'll take care of the boys tonight." She gathered Matthew and Timmy's hands. "Say good night, boys. Miechael, see you tomorrow."

Timmy dragged his foot. He wanted to speak, but bit his lip.

They were almost to the bedrooms, but the hall carried Louise's voice. "I'll read to you after you bathe."

"Can I pick out the book, Grandma?"

"Yes, you may, Timmy. And, boys, wash behind your ears and brush your teeth. Do you need my assistance?"

Timmy said, "I'm in the shower, Grandma. I have every-thing—a towel, a cloth, and soap to wash. I can't hear you."

"Grandma, will you come and shut the water off?" Matthew called out. "The tub is getting full, and I can't turn the knob."

"Coming, Matthew."

Louise saw the bubbles and tried turning the knob with the water running, but her hands kept slipping. "Matthew, what did you do?"

Matthew began giggling. He had covered the knob with soap.

Louise reached and grabbed for a towel. "I think you're done in here, Matthew." She pulled the plug, and only the gurgle of water draining could be heard.

Claudia stretched, and it looked like an exaggerated yawn. "Where am I bunking down, Sara?"

"I'll show you."

Ken grazed Sara's shoulder. "I'm going out to check the barn and Sam. I'll be right in. Up for a stroll when I get back?" He winked as he lifted his Stetson.

She listened as the door closed. Her heart was still fluttering from his look. Sara heard Claudia shift. Together, arm in arm, they climbed the steps.

Sara gathered the items. "Claudia, here's some towels, wash-rags, and toiletries. The shower is down the hall on the right, and the claw tub is to the left. Enjoy. Your room is the one straight across from ours. Night, Clo."

Sara paused until she heard the water running and some kind of gargling. She hoped it wasn't Claudia trying to sing.

"Good night, baby birl."

Sara walked the hall, checking on Miechael and then her boys. Matthew was fast asleep. She stepped to Timmy's bed and touched his forehead.

He whispered, "Mommy, do you think we could have a girl sister like Luci?"

Sara was taken off guard. Where had that come from? She cleared her throat. "I'll speak with your father about that." She tucked the blanket around his shoulders and blew him a kiss. "Sleep tight, Timmy. I love you."

Sara gingerly walked downstairs and cleared the game away. She hurriedly straightened and fluffed the pillows in the living room. Ken hadn't come inside, so she checked the office's message machine. She was talking in the air as she penned down the messages. Karen had three shows and had sold fourteen purses, and the check was to arrive a week from today in the amount.

She suddenly shivered and hit the Save button, for Ken was blowing in her ear and was nuzzling the back of her neck.

"Need any help?" he asked.

Sara felt her nerve endings electrify as he placed his arms around her middle and blew again in her ear. She turned, tipping her head. He gently gave her a slow, soft kiss. She tried to rise, but her legs wouldn't cooperate. They were weak. She placed a hand on his chest, and he shuddered then moaned.

Sara let out an unsteady breath. "Ken, let's take that walk."

His eyes widened, and were darker than coal. A slight gradual smile formed at his lips. He took her small hand in his. "Sara, what's on your mind? Is there anything troubling you? You seem mighty antsy."

Sara pointed at the moon. She shakily said, "Look, the moon appears low, and it is so full." It was orange, and the enchantment filled the sky.

"Sara, it's a harvest moon, just like it was the night I proposed to you." He nodded. "The stars are bright, and they seemed to be addressing us. They are winking."

She squeezed his hand a little harder and pressed it to her lips. "There's something I want—I *need* to tell you." She paused then blurted out, "Luke asked me tonight if he could have a sister like Luci."

Ken wrapped his arm around Sara's shoulder and drew her near.

"Ken?"

"I'm listening, sweetheart."

"Well, Ken, it's hard for me to stay focused when you're doing that. You're so near."

Ken's smile deepened, and his dimple showed. His eyes were twinkling. "My mother raised me as a gentleman." He dropped his hands to his sides and took a step from her. "Is that better?"

Her mind was mush. *Think, Sara.*

They continued walking, and entered the swing area. He bowed and pointed for her to sit. She obeyed. He stayed at a distance but gave Sara a kiss. He then took the swing and gave her a push and then another. She saw how noble, kind, and patient he was being with her. He hadn't rushed her to speak, and for that, Sara was grateful.

She looked up at the sky and thought, *Lord, thank you for Ken, my children, our friends, and for the new family members. May we come together and remember You always.*

She felt a tapping on her shoulder and then a soft stroke on her cheek.

"Sara, where did you go?" He stopped the swing and gazed down at her.

A breeze whizzed by, moving her ebony curls. He entwined his fingers in her locks. He was too close. Sara pulled the letter from her forgotten apron pocket and showed Ken. "Your sister is reaching out to me."

"It seems, but you haven't read it?"

She bunched her brow. "Ken, I've been a little busy."

Ken laughed and gave her a hug. "Isn't it wonderful, Sara? We have made a complete journey, and it led us back together." He breathed deeply and inhaled the scent of her hair. The citrus smell lingered. His eyes beckoned, and slowly, their eyes locked.

She let out a breath. "I can't think of anywhere else I would rather be."

"Sara, do you know how much I care for you?" He paused, bringing her closer. "I'm hopelessly devoted and in love with you."

Sara reached for his hand, stepping away, and began walking. She appreciated this quiet time they were sharing, yet she could hardly speak. She paused. "Ken, I feel your love in your breath, your move, your smile. It's stamped all over you. I've been more blessed than most women. You show and have shown me a love only God can instill in man."

She let go of his hand and raised a finger to his mouth. "I will honor you, and I trust you with my life." A tear slid down her face.

He used his finger and lightly touched her face, removing the tear.

Sara continued. "You confirmed your love for me in other ways also. It's in the way you've accepted my mom, and we know her tactics." She let out a long rushing sigh, placing a hand to his chest. "Ken, watching you with our children, showing your tenderness, then the way you accepted responsibility with your nephew, Miechael, and your understanding with your sister, Mariah. Also, don't let me leave out your fairness with your father, Jon. Ken, you have calmly and openheartedly received his apologies and affections."

Sara noticed when Ken turned slightly that his eyes were moist. He held her. "My beloved, you are as fine as precious gold that's been refined. I can scarcely take in the air around me." He wiped Sara's tears away and drew her nearer.

Sara stood on tiptoes and gave Ken a kiss. They dallied. She placed her hand in his and at a snail's pace began walking toward the house. She broke contact only long enough to reach for the door handle on the back door.

Sara paused, twisting on the step, meeting Ken at eye level, and gazed at him. Their eyes searched, met, and locked. Sara seized both of Ken's hands. In her excitement, she swung them back and forth. His head titled, and his mouth smirked.

"Ken, I-I have a doctor's appointment on Monday."

He arched his brows to his hairline and lifted Sara away from him. "What's wrong?"

She shyly smiled as a blush came from her neck to her face. "Nothing is wrong. Everything is right, I think."

Ken held his pose.

Sara continued. "Remember how we passed the time my first night back, cowboy?"

His eyes brightened and twinkled.

"You know, coming home from Claudia's? Well, my love, we are having a new beginning." She didn't wait but turned and pulled him through the door. She broke hands only long enough to light a candle. She motioned with her forefinger for him to follow in silence and to shut the door.

Ken grabbed her arm. He went weak; he had to let her lead. Hand in hand, they walked quietly through the house and took the stairs. She stopped outside their bedroom and searched his eyes. "Hey, cowboy, want me to snuff the wick?"

He removed his hat and lowered his hand to her back and pushed their bedroom door open. The floor squeaked, and she snickered. He paused and searched her face as he brushed her lips and then tapped her bottom.

Sara tilted her head from side to side to listen as he padded away. He said nothing as he used the candle, being their only light. Sara let a little giggle escape when she heard his boot hit the door.

21

The next morning was a bustling time. Claudia had awakened early and surprisingly made coffee for Ken, Sam, and herself.

It looked powerful in her cup. The boys were sitting at the kitchen table, finishing their oh-so-hard eggs and toast.

"Hi, baby girl," Claudia greeted.

"Good morning, Clo." Sara rubbed her eyes.

"I made you toast and hot tea. Come sit."

Sara considered for a moment. It sure was nice to be waited on for a change. Sara bowed her head in thanks, took a bite of toast, and graciously sipped the steaming drink of tea. Ooo. The tea was horrible. She tried not to spit it out. Not only was it lacking sugar, but also sugar would not have helped. Sara thought it could have been unsweetened thick molasses; it was difficult to handle. Sara began coughing, and caught a glimpse of Claudia's questioning eyes. She came over and pounded Sara on the back.

"You okay? Did it go down the wrong way?"

Sara gave a weak smile and a shaky nod.

Claudia captured a seat. "Sara, I brought Ken a real prize winner. When his filly is bred, her foal or foals should be of the highest quality, one which would bring a huge sum if he were to sell it, but we've come to terms. Shucks, Sara, this will be an added beginning for your horse farm. Now there's no easy way to say this, but his other mares aren't worth a hoot. They're only good for a riding or working horse. Do not breed them if he wants a higher-end return."

Claudia crossed her legs and said, "When I was walking the farm, Sara, I saw there was empty unclaimed land. A riding course could be mapped out. You know people pay to ride. Well, it's a thought for when Ken retires from the banking business some year."

Claudia stood up and stretched. "Sara, I was wondering." She rubbed her chin. "How did you ever start into a purse business? We never talked about it when you stayed with me. Do you have any recruits, and what are your plans with your income you're making?"

Sara's mouth opened at Claudia's raw bluntness, but she respectfully answered. "I've always liked to sew Claudia. I began making a few purses and gave them away as gifts. Some of the recipients gave me compliments and requested me to make purses for them at different times so they could buy and use them for gifts."

Sara folded her hands. "Ken and I talked about my purses, and he saw how successful my designs were, so he suggested I consider moving forward and take an opportunity on a new business venture. He advised me on how to structure reading charts and recommended I should call and set up an appointment with Jud to see if I would qualify for a business loan. You know with Ken being family, he was not allowed to offer me a loan, Claudia."

Claudia kept shaking her head. "So when we met on the plane, you were on your way back home from your meeting with Jud?"

Sara rinsed her cup and made new tea. "Yes. I also had finished a visit with his wife. She's my best friend, and would you believe, Karen became my first recruit. Claudia, she's so nice."

Sara patted Claudia on the shoulder. "As for the money, Claudia, I don't have a vision outside paying off the bank loan and keeping in supplies. I really didn't expect my business would grow this fast or that sales would be so great. Do you have any ideas?"

Claudia pushed her hat back and stroked her chin. "Sara, let me think on it. I may have an idea or two."

The ladies chatted as they walked to the barn. Sam and Ken had anchored Velvety. They had primed her for breeding. Sam and Ken assured Claudia that every precaution had been taken for the horse's safety. Now they would just have to wait and see if the studding worked.

Ken and Sam looked on as Sara surprisingly spurted out, "Claudia, have you called Karen and made arrangements about you and Jack?"

Claudia sidestepped as her red face softened. Then a voice as gentle as her words came. "Sara, he's wrote me, a lot." She dug into her new handbag that Sara had given her and pulled out a stack of letters. Flapping them in the air, she went on, "He's written all these letters since you and I've last talked. I should be so worthy. Ain't he something?"

Sara's eyes widened, and she stared on.

Claudia clasped her fists to her heart and continued. "I told you about my past, and it ain't a winner. I'm petrified. You know I'm not a young spring chicken anymore and hardly the feminine type with makeup, dresses, heels, and all."

She added, "What if we did progress as a couple? How would we be able to—well, there's things to overcome like careers and where to live, and our monies. Could we handle all this?"

Claudia was pacing, and her arms were flying outward. "On top of that, Sara, there would be the meeting of a new person as in a chaperone. You know I ain't no good with meeting people. Besides, they would be watching me, and that ain't no good either. And there would be tension with Jack and me courting. Thanks for caring, baby girl."

Claudia shifted her weight. "Jack is a fine, noble man, and very honorable." She patted her letters and stuffed them back into the purse, nodding. "No, I think I'll let it ride for now."

Sara placed a hand on Claudia's arm. "Claudia, are you being fair to Jack? You're all worked up. Let me help you. Want me to call Karen before you leave? We can put Karen on speakerphone. What do you say, Claudia? It's the least I can do for you after all you've done for me. Jack deserves a chance." She nudged Claudia's elbow. "Let's go into my office. It is more private there."

There was another pause. Claudia's lips trembled as she linked arms with Sara.

Sara dialed Karen's phone number. "Hello, Karen. This is Sara. I'm placing you on speakerphone. I have with me standing here, Claudia. Karen, I understand Jack has continued writing to Claudia, and now he wants a courtship with Miss Claudia. She needs to come to Ohio, and she knows no one else and will need a place to properly stay. Karen, you know how the procedures in courting works, and she needs your help, so here's Claudia for any questions either one of you may have. Be easy on her."

"Hello, Karen?" Claudia said.

The two spoke, and many questions were answered. Karen left Claudia an open invitation to come to Ohio and have a stay at the bed-and-breakfast. Karen assured her they could and would work everything out. She just needed to be called in advance.

Sara looked up and said, "Here, take this." She handed Claudia a typed letter of intent.

They moved from the office, and they journeyed toward the truck. They patted hands and had a better understanding of each other woman to woman.

At the truck, Sara and Claudia held hands as Sara prayed for safety and for God's will in both their lives. After a few more hugs, and with both of them being a little teary-eyed, they made promises to keep in touch.

"Baby girl, I'm glad you're doing well and that you are truly happy." Claudia took another step and waved to Sam and punched Ken in the arm. "Let me know how the stallion works out for you. I'll be looking for your call." She pulled Ken close. "Take care of baby girl, or you'll have me to deal with."

Claudia adjusted her hat, sniffed, and wiped her nose on her sleeve. She climbed into the truck. One last wave was given before Claudia blew her horn and shifted her truck into drive.

Sara and Ken stood arm in arm and watched long after the truck was driven down the lane and only a trail of dust remained in the air. The midmorning sun's rays were already strong. Sara motioned for Sam and the boys to return back to the barn as Ken winked and joined Sam. Sara hugged her mom and watched her go into the house, batting at her apron.

Sara walked until she came to the hay wagon. The back was open, and she jumped up. Looking around the farm, she realized she wanted to enjoy and take a moment to reflect. How thankful she was for Claudia's skill and care. To have her visit and show kindness, generosity, and for her trust. Most of all for the wonderful friendship they had formed.

Sara giggled and thought about her best friend, Karen, and that crazy penny swear necklace, and for her friend's husband, Jud, who took a chance on her business venture. For Ken's parents, their love and the giving of their time. And for Jack's time and support. Her mother, the way she loved unconditionally.

The circle of her life had joined together, with others willingly putting their lives on hold and helping mold her life back. It was a complete circle.

Sara stretched. She thought she must thank these people, one for her mother's uprooting where she lived most of her life to come live with them. For her understanding and faithful love. And then her sweet husband, Ken, for his patience, love, and support. His openness with the family and their children, but most of all for how wonderful it was to have her adventures with his consent and know she was never left alone.

Yes, she was thankful for her upbringing and blessed for Ken's strong belief in God. *He cares, He most divinely cares. My savior has been there from the beginning.*

"Sara?"

She turned and looked toward the voice.

Her mother was flagging her into the house. "The lunch is brewing. It's vegetable soup. It should be done in two hours." Louise fluffed up her apron. "Sam would like to take Miechael and the boys and me for a hike and do some fishing at the pond. I was going to make a picnic lunch for us." Turning a little pink, she asked, "Is it okay for them to go with us?"

Sara looked at her and flexed her toes so as not to laugh. "Sure, Mom. They will enjoy the adventure, and I'm sure you will. You two be careful."

Sara worked until the noon hour. The sky had turned from the brightly lit morning to blackening clouds, which promised to threaten and break through. She did a mental checkoff. *I have all the shows entered and the totals of the benefits completed.*

Sitting there, she smiled at the great success her business had grown into. She decided to make a list of things to find out. *If Karen had all the shows recorded and I need to call her and see if any booked shows were still outstanding. I need to pen a thank-you note to Jud saying thanks for all his help. One to Jack for his time invested in helping me to remember life before and its values. Oh yes, a thank-you note to Donald for his perseverance in finding me. For Ken's mother and father and all their help.*

As she stood, she patted the apron pocket. There was the forgotten letter from Mariah. She clutched it to her chest. Ripping it open, she read the text:

> Life is funny. I was looking for my stepfather, which turned out is my adoptive dad. I'm not strong in faith, but God has His timing and His ways. I'm sure my mother can handle anything or anyone who comes her way. Isn't she awesome?
>
> Now your husband is something else. He's so easy to talk to, and I greatly appreciate his concern for Miechael and myself. I think Ken's a keeper, but don't tell him I said so.
>
> Sara, my dear, you are such a blessing in a storm. Thanks for the letter and purse. I do want us to keep in

touch. I've a fondness toward you. Thanks for caring for my precious boy. Keep him in line. I'll call soon, and give Ken my address should he care to correspond.

Sincerely,
Your newly found sister, Mariah

Sara dabbed at her eyes and folded her hands. She had a fresh hope of a new beginning of things to come. She touched her penny swear necklace and slipped it off. She now had two treasures.

Sara went into the house to her room. She lifted the candied-pink-lined box and placed the necklace on one side and placed the letter from Mariah in the hidden compartment underneath.

Sara giggled when she saw the note from Claudia calling her baby girl and leaving her number and telling her to call for it was already in the box. She tapped the box's top and bowed. *Please watch over my friend, Claudia; my best friend, Karen; and my newly found sister, Mariah. Let us accept Your will and worship You.*

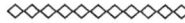

Lunch was over, and dinner was well into the evening's making. Sam had called and asked if it were all right if he and Louise were to take the boys into town for a movie. They would treat them to ice cream at the parlor shop. Of course Sara had agreed. Sam was a kind and thoughtful man plus her mother seemed happy again.

Sara turned the fire on low and went to the barn. "Ken!" she yelled.

He pushed his hat back on his head and was grinning. "What brings me this pleasure?"

She held out her hand with a fresh glass of ice tea. "Thought you might be thirsty, cowboy."

He gladly took the beverage and seemed to inhale it. "Thanks. Want to watch as I finish up the chores? We can still get in a ride, only using the other mare, not Velvety."

"How is she doing?"

"Velvety is adjusting, but she's spoiled." Ken tossed the straw around the stalls and fed the last few animals. He turned. "Ready for the ride?"

His smile was breathtaking. Even though he was sweaty and a little smelly, she nodded. It was soon they were saddled in, looking over the property.

Sara listened as he raved about the richness of the land and how God had blessed him. They nudged the horses and trotted around the entire fencerow. They laughed, joked, and talked. It was wonderful just having the time alone with him. She realized she had taken their life for granted. She had allowed her marriage to become unfulfilling before her accident.

The rebuilding and reknowing of Ken had brought all the flooding feelings and thoughts on how she first felt when they met at the Bible study on a Wednesday night many years ago.

She couldn't get enough of his sight then, and certainly not now. He was sitting tall in the saddle. Those broad shoulders and self-assurance that set in his jaw. His powerful tanned arms and muscles flexing as he rode. His hair flowing and those eyes of coal.

"Sara, you appeared to be far away," Ken said. "Where did you go?"

"Nowhere. I'm here." Sara blushed. *Yes, I like his smile as well as his soothing husky voice.* "Let's ride home, my love."

"Yes. Let's."

Their eyes met momentarily, and willingness and a real desire came upon Sara. Ken leaned over in the saddle and gave her a kiss. He began soft then deepened. She felt his energy as he broke the kiss. He swatted her horse and his, then they rode like the dickens to the barn. They silently dismounted and hurriedly brushed the horses down. Ken smacked the horses' bottoms, urging them into their stalls.

Neither her mother, Sam, nor the boys had returned. She stood and shyly offered her hand. He was so obliging. As he whisked Sara into his arms, ever so tenderly, the smoldering look she had come to appreciate appeared in his eyes, and from his body language, she knew this was the place and adventure she wanted to share for the rest of her life—with only him.

Ken edged Sara down to him, lowering her to his level. Their lips touched with a memorable kiss. And his kiss lingered.

www.ingramcontent.com/pod-product-compliance
Lightning Source LLC
Chambersburg PA
CBHW051650260626
47170CB00004B/1428